BELMONT COUNTY D.L. (MFP)

3 3667 00442 9582

P9-DFM-565

FIC BYB Large Print
Wife by Wednesday
Bybee, Catherine,
33667004429582
BELMONT COUNTY DIST LIBRARY
MFP   06/2016

Wife by Wednesday

Center Point
Large Print

**This Large Print Book carries the
Seal of Approval of N.A.V.H.**

Wife by Wednesday

Catherine Bybee

CENTER POINT LARGE PRINT
THORNDIKE, MAINE

This Center Point Large Print edition
is published in the year 2016 by arrangement with
Amazon Publishing, www.apub.com.

Copyright © 2011 by Catherine Bybee.

All rights reserved.

Originally published in the United States
by Amazon Publishing, 2011.

This is a work of fiction. Names, characters, places,
and incidents are either the product of the author's
imagination or are used fictitiously, and any resemblance
to actual persons living or dead, business establishments,
events, or locales, is entirely coincidental.

The text of this Large Print edition is unabridged.
In other aspects, this book may vary
from the original edition.
Printed in the United States of America
on permanent paper.
Set in 16-point Times New Roman type.

ISBN: 978-1-62899-988-4

Library of Congress Cataloging-in-Publication Data

Names: Bybee, Catherine, author.
Title: Wife by Wednesday / Catherine Bybee.
Description: Center Point Large Print edition. | Thorndike, Maine :
Center Point Large Print, 2016. | ©2011
Identifiers: LCCN 2016010596 | ISBN 9781628999884
   (hardcover : alk. paper)
Subjects: LCSH: Arranged marriage—Fiction. | Large type books.
Classification: LCC PS3602.Y344 W54 2016 | DDC 813/.6—dc23
LC record available at http://lccn.loc.gov/2016010596

This one is for my dad, who has read every word
I've ever written and still looks me in the eye.
Thank you for your never-ending support.
I love you!

Chapter One

"I need a wife, Carter, and I needed her yesterday." Riding in the back of the town car, en route to a Starbucks, of all places, Blake Harrison glanced at his watch for the tenth time that hour.

Carter's startled laugh rode on Blake's last nerve. "Then pick one of the masses and walk the aisle."

His best friend's offhand advice might have held merit if Blake could trust the women in his life. Sadly, he couldn't. "And risk losing everything? You know me better than that. I don't need emotion clogging up something as important as a marriage agreement." An agreement was exactly what he needed. A contract. A business deal that would benefit both parties for the course of one year. Then they could go their separate ways and never lay eyes on each other again.

"Some of the women you show up with would be happy to sign a prenuptial agreement."

He'd already thought of that. But he'd worked hard for his emotionless-bastard reputation and didn't need to mess it up by pretending he was in love in order to have a woman walk up the courtroom steps with him. "I need someone who's on board with my plan, someone I'm not remotely attracted to."

"You sure this dating service is the right way to go?"

"Matchmaking, not dating."

"What's the difference?"

"They don't match your love interests. They match your life plan."

"How romantic." Carter's sarcasm came across like a shout.

"I'm not the only one in my position, apparently."

Carter laughed and then choked on his own breath. "Really," he sputtered. "I don't know any other men with your title and your wealth calling a stranger to set them up."

"This guy comes highly recommended, a businessman helping men like me in similar situations."

"What's his name?"

"Sam Elliot."

"Never heard of him."

Traffic clogged the intersection two blocks from where his appointment with said businessman was taking place. The seconds clicked past the time of his scheduled appointment. Damn, he hated being late.

"I gotta go."

"I hope you know what you're doing."

"Business is what I do, Carter."

His friend huffed in disapproval. "I know. It's relationships you suck at."

"Screw you." But Blake knew his friend was right.

"You're not my type."

Blake's driver swerved in traffic to make a light. Ruthless, just like his boss wanted him. "See you tonight for drinks."

Blake hung up the phone, slipped it into the pocket of his dress coat, and sat back in his seat. So he was late. Men in his position could walk in half past the designated hour and still have people climbing over themselves to make it look like it was their fault. A lot was riding on the outcome of this meeting. Finding a wife before the week was out in order to keep the ancestral home that went with his title—not to mention the remainder of his father's fortune—hinged on Sam Elliot.

He hoped to hell that his personal assistant's contact knew what he was talking about. Otherwise, Blake might be forced to broach the subject of marriage to Jacqueline, or maybe Vanessa. Jacqueline loved her independence more than his money. The fact that she kept a lover other than him pushed her out of the running for wife. That left Vanessa. Beautiful, blonde, and already riding the wave of soon-to-be ex because of her hints about being exclusive. He didn't like the thought of leading her on. He was a bastard, but never cruel. Some women would disagree, and the tabloids had branded him pompous and cunning. If the papers sniffed around what he was doing, they'd write it up and turn it into a joke. He'd like to avoid the added scandal. Reality, however, was a rightful bitch, and he knew his fake marriage would need to look real in order to keep his father's lawyers satisfied.

Neil pulled the long black car up to the curb and quickly opened Blake's door in front of the green-and-white-painted coffeehouse. With brief-case in hand, Blake ignored the turned heads when he strode inside the storefront. The rich smell of freshly ground beans filled his nose as he scanned the tables searching for the man he pictured as Sam Elliot. Blake assumed he'd find a man wearing a business suit and carrying a portfolio filled with files of wifely prospects inside.

The first glance didn't deliver, so he removed his sunglasses and started over. A young couple with dueling laptops sipped their lattes across from each other at one small table. At another, a man in crew shorts and a T-shirt argued with someone on his cell phone. At the counter ordering was a couple pushing a stroller. Stepping farther inside, Blake noticed the small frame of the back of a woman with a mass of curly auburn hair. Her toe tapped anxiously, or maybe she was listening to music through a set of earbuds. With his eyes still skimming the small crowd, Blake found a lone man occupying a plush chair. He wore a casual pair of pants and looked to be in his late forties. Instead of a briefcase, the man held a book. Blake narrowed his eyes and caught the other man's attention. Instead of a flicker of understanding, the man's dark gaze fell back to his book.

Damn, maybe Mr. Elliot was caught in the same traffic.

Late never boded well for prospective clients, no matter what business they were in.

If Blake had another choice, he would've turned and left.

Walking past the lone redhead, Blake stepped around the stroller and ordered a plain coffee, then resigned himself to sit for a few minutes and wait. He placed his briefcase on an empty table and turned to get his coffee when the teenage kid behind the counter called his name.

The hard weight of someone's stare rolled down his spine. His eyes scanned around the room to see who was watching. Instantly, a set of emerald-green eyes narrowed as they took him in. The petite woman sitting alone wasn't listening to music or reading a magazine. She was staring directly at him.

Her striking gaze returned to a small notebook computer before bouncing back his way. A flicker of recognition fell over her. He'd seen the expression before whenever someone placed his name with his image. Here in California, the frequency of that awareness didn't happen as often as it did at home, but Blake recognized it nonetheless.

The woman seemed harmless enough. That was

until she opened her mouth and spoke directly to him. "You're late."

Two words. It took two words, in a voice so low it dripped like sin and put phone sex operators to shame, to render Blake speechless.

Red's words registered. "Excuse me?"

"You are Mr. Harrison, right?"

The question was simple, but Blake couldn't quite comprehend it. He answered on autopilot, completely derailed by the woman in front of him. "I am."

She stood and only met the top of his shoulder. "Sam Elliot," she introduced herself and stuck out her hand for him to shake.

It wasn't often that Blake was kicked back a few notches. Yet, with only a couple of words, the woman in front of him had done so. He reached out and took her hand in his and a wave of heat surged over him. Her penetrating stare and knowing smile wavered when they shook hands. Her palm was cool, even if her demeanor was one of complete control.

"You're not a man." Blake wanted to groan. That had to be the most stupid thing he'd ever said to a woman in his life.

Ms. Elliot, however, was nonchalant. "Never have been." She offered him a smile and exposed perfect teeth as she removed her hand from his. He missed it instantly.

"I was expecting a man."

"I get that a lot. Most of the time, it works to my advantage." She indicated the chair across from her. "Would you like to sit so we can get started?"

He hesitated, not sure if he should continue this "interview" or insist on the woman's gender to change. He didn't consider himself sexist, but musing over the woman taking her seat and crossing her slacks-covered legs drew his attention away from his goal and placed it squarely on her. Sam Elliot could be considered the poster child for contradiction, and Blake hadn't learned anything about the woman yet.

He would give her ten minutes to prove she could meet his needs. If she didn't, he'd move on and explore other options.

Blake unbuttoned the top button on his suit jacket before taking his place at the table. "Is Sam short for Samantha?"

"Yes." Samantha didn't meet his eyes as she removed a stack of papers from a small case she'd placed against the side of her chair. The brief smile she'd given him was gone, replaced with an unrevealing thin line between her lips.

"Do you use 'Sam' to fool your clients?"

Her hand stalled as she pushed the stack of papers in his direction. "Would you have come if you knew I was a woman?"

Probably not. Without voicing his words, he watched her.

Samantha tilted her head to the side and continued. "You make my case, Mr. Harrison. Let me see if I'm reading your intentions. In your mind, you've set a time limit for me to prove myself. What was it? Twenty minutes?"

"Ten," he blurted out, not meaning to. What was it about this woman with the bedroom voice that stole his ability to hold his tongue?

She smiled again and his stomach knotted with a shot of unexpected and unwanted desire.

"Ten minutes," she repeated. "To outline exactly how I plan on finding you the perfect wife for your short-term goals. A businessman like yourself expects quick efficiency and no emotional baggage to complicate matters." She watched him, her green eyes never wavering. Her pert, freckled nose looked too innocent above those delicious pink lips while she delivered her words in that erotic 900-number voice. "Am I right so far?"

"Completely."

"Women are emotional, which is why your assistant looked into my service to begin with. My guess is, there are many women who would sell their souls to marry you, Mr. Harrison, but you don't trust them enough to give them the title."

Most of the time, it was him outlining his needs. Having the tables reversed should have left him feeling exposed. Somehow, listening to Sam Elliot, who was definitely not a man, spell out his dilemma didn't strip him bare. Instead, he felt blanketed in comfort. He'd come to the right place to fix his problem.

"How do I know I can trust a woman you come up with?"

"I prescreen every prospect in my directory just as thoroughly as the client. Detailed background checks expose financial obligations, personal habits, and any family skeletons hiding in closets."

"You sound like a private investigator."

"Not hardly. But I can understand why you'd think that. Matching people is what I do."

Blake sat back and crossed his hands over his chest. He liked her, he decided, mentally adding another ten minutes to his predetermined time.

"Shall we continue?"

He reached for his coffee and nodded.

Sam grasped a pen and twisted the papers she'd pushed in front of him back her way. "I have a few questions for you before *I allow* this to move forward."

Blake's brow rose with her words. Interesting. "How long do I have to prove myself to you, Ms. Elliot?"

She glanced up through long lashes. "Five minutes."

He sat forward, thoroughly intrigued with what she was going to determine about him in that amount of time.

"Have you ever been arrested?"

His record was clear, but that wasn't the question.

He knew if he lied to Sam, she'd pack up her things and walk out the door. "I was seventeen, and the kid I punched was hitting on my sister. The record was buried." As were all the records of children from his station in life.

"Have you ever hit a woman?"

His jaw tightened. "Never."

"Ever wanted to?" She watched him now, eyes sharp.

"No." Violence didn't play into his personality.

"I need the name of your closest friend."

"Carter Billings."

She scribbled down the name.

"Worst enemy?"

He didn't see that question coming. "I'm not sure how to answer that."

"Let me rephrase it, then. Who in your life would like to see you come to harm?"

His first thoughts scanned his list of business associates who might have felt slighted over the years. None would be better off if he were gone at this point. There was only one person who might see things differently.

"Whose image are you thinking of, Mr. Harrison?"

Blake took a drink of his coffee and felt it hit the bottom of his stomach with a thump. "Only one."

Samantha lifted her eyes to his, waiting.

"My cousin, Howard Walker."

A tiny slack in her jaw, a slump in her shoulders,

these were the only things that indicated the impact of his words. Much to Blake's surprise, Samantha Elliot wrote down the information and didn't question further.

She removed the top sheet of her papers and handed him the others. "I'm going to need you to fill these out. You can fax them to me at the number on the bottom of page eight."

"Did I pass your test, Ms. Elliot?"

"Honesty needs to be maintained throughout this process. So far, everything is working for me."

It was Blake's turn to smile. "I could have lied about the assault charge."

Samantha started to pack up her things as she spoke. "His name was Drew Falsworth. You were two months past your seventeenth birthday when you broke his nose at a polo match at the prep school you both attended. Drew had a reputation for dating girls long enough to get them into bed before dumping and moving on to the next. Your sister was smart to stay away. If you hadn't hit the bastard to protect your sister, or lied to me and I'd found out about it, this interview would have been over before you even sat down."

"How the hell—"

"I have a very extensive list of contacts. Most of which I'm sure you'll know about before this day is out."

Damn right. He'd be on the phone with his assistant before he reached the car.

"What's this going to cost me, Ms. Elliot?"

"Consider me an agent. When your lawyer draws up the prenuptial agreement, bear in mind that twenty percent of what you offer your future wife will be paid to me up front."

"And if I only offer her a small stipend?"

"The women I work with have a minimum spelled out in that stack of papers."

"And if the woman doesn't hold to her end of the deal? If she fights the contract after a year?"

Samantha stood, giving Blake no choice but to stand beside her.

"She won't."

"You sound so certain."

"The predetermined amount of money, her share, goes into an account. If the woman fights for more, that money pays your attorneys to squelch her. Anything left over is yours to keep. The only time this would change is if a child entered into the picture and paternity tests proved it was yours. Family courts with kids aren't something I agree to deal with. It will be up to you to keep it in your pants, Mr. Harrison—that is, of course, if you intend to end the marriage after the agreed-upon year. If not, then enjoy your happily ever after and name your child after me."

She'd thought of everything. To say he was impressed was an understatement.

"I need those papers by three this afternoon. I'll be in touch by five with a list of prospective women. We'll set up meetings as soon as tomorrow if your schedule allows."

Blake reached down, lifted her bag, and handed it to her.

She shoved a lock of unruly hair from her eyes and swung the handle over her shoulder. "Do you have any more questions for me, Mr. Harrison? Or should I be calling you 'Your Grace'?"

The slow way she rolled his title off her tongue with her hypnotic voice was something he could get used to. He wouldn't mind hearing it again, over the phone . . . "How about Blake?"

As soon as Sam knew she wasn't being watched, she slid behind the wheel of her car and allowed the Cheshire cat grin she'd been feeling deep inside her to spread over her face. An undignified Snoopy dance had her wiggling her butt in the soft leather. "About friggin' time," she whispered to herself.

The dashing duke was her ticket to the big leagues. From the inception of Alliance, she'd pictured clients like Blake Harrison lining up for her services—rich men in need of finding a wife to check off their bucket list. She found wives for men who didn't have time or the desire to go through the dating game. They weren't looking for love, but companionship. Some men wanted a wife so their lovers would stop bugging them for a ring. To date, she had plenty of personal referrals that were helping her build her business and a steady income to sustain her.

With Harrison, and his estimated profit potential, she'd be able to pay her largest expense for a good two to three years. Or so she hoped.

A millionaire on his own, Harrison didn't need his late father's money. But if he permitted a bank account large enough to purchase a small country to disappear into the melting pot of charity or to the cousin Blake had mentioned, that would be a shame. With all the corruption and scandal associated with charities, there was no telling where that money would end up or whose pockets it would fatten.

Sam knew firsthand how do-good money often fell into greedy hands. Harrison's situation would bring up distractions she'd not faced before. His title might be the biggest problem to overcome. She'd have to screen the prospective women to make sure they didn't have fairy-tale dreams of becoming a duchess. Years of Disney videos were hard to combat, and combined with Harrison's over-the-top good looks, the women would have to be blind not to want more from the man than his money or title.

The pictures she'd seen of him didn't do him justice. She'd always looked up to men, had to with her five-foot-five frame, but Blake was six-one on a bad day, with shoulders rippling with muscles. She'd seen tabloid pictures of him on a beach in Tahiti that hinted at the physique hiding beneath his suit. When he'd walked into the coffee shop, all eyes turned to him, yet he didn't even notice. He simply scanned the room looking for her. With any other client, she'd have taken to her feet the second he hit the door, but with Blake, she'd needed a minute to compose herself. His firm, rugged jaw and striking gray eyes had penetrated her normally calm disposition and made her heart leap.

His looks would be a distraction. It would be best for all involved if the woman he picked to be his wife lived in one country while he lived in another. Spending long amounts of time with him would tempt any woman with a pulse to sleep with him.

Sam removed her cell phone from her purse and called her assistant.

"Alliance, this is Eliza."

"Hey, it's me."

"How did it go?" Eliza jumped right in with her query.

"Perfectly. Did you pull the files and make the calls?"

"I did. Joanne was the only woman not available at this time."

Sam pictured the tall brunette. "Really? Why?"

"Has a boyfriend, apparently."

That did tend to mess up marriage to another man. Without Joanne, there were three other perfect candidates. Unless Blake had a problem with beautiful women, she'd have the man a wife by Wednesday. It was only Monday.

"Her loss."

"Are you coming in?"

"I have an errand to run, and then I'll be there."

"Bring lunch."

Eliza and Sam had been friends for some time, long before their business relationship took off. "As your boss, shouldn't you be picking up lunch for me?" she teased.

"Not when my slave-driving employer isn't in the office long enough to man the phones." The office—what a joke. Sam used the spare bedroom in the town house.

Laughing, Sam said, "I'll be there in half an hour."

"You might want to call Moonlight first."

Sam sat a little taller. "Why? Is something wrong?" Worry wiggled around in her stomach, producing a familiar sense of panic.

"Nothing urgent. Jordan isn't eating as much as they'd like. They thought you should stop by and talk to her."

Samantha blew out a long-suffering breath and forced her shoulders to relax. "OK." Her plans for the afternoon would now be complicated with a side trip to the extended care facility taking care of her younger sister. The last time Jordan had stopped eating, she ended up in the hospital suffering with an infection that spread throughout her bloodstream. Sam hoped her sister was depressed and not ill. Sad that those were the top choices for why Jordan wasn't eating.

But what else was there? Depression had led to Jordan's attempted suicide that resulted in a stroke instead of death. "I'll be late, but if you can wait, I'll bring lunch."

"Let me know if you get tied up."

"I will. Thanks."

Sam hung up, started her car, and pointed it toward Moonlight Villas. The exclusive home cost over a hundred grand a year and was the reason Samantha needed the income a deal with Blake Harrison would bring. She was a month behind on her personal bills and always cutting the checks to Moonlight a week or two late. The last thing Sam wanted was to crumble under financial pressure and end up having to put Jordan in a state-run facility. She'd be ignored in those homes and likely end up with bedsores and untreatable infections within a month. No, Sam would live out of her car before she'd let that happen.

Picturing the duke, Sam knew things wouldn't end up in such dire straits. He stood to lose close to three hundred million from his father's estate if he didn't marry by the end of the month. Blake would likely pay the woman walking down the aisle a nice chunk and therefore pay Alliance enough to float for some time. All Sam had to do was fluff up the women in line and make sure none of them hit any panic buttons.

Easy peasy. Or so she hoped.

Chapter Two

*B*lake fingered the photographs and files of the three women Samantha had sent his way. Each one was perfect. They were educated, cultured, and beautiful. So why the hell were they registered with a dating service to find a temporary husband? There had to be a link between them and Miss Matchmaker herself, but Blake wasn't seeing it.

Candidate No. 1, Candice . . . No last name. According to the portfolio, she was a second-year law student with typical educational loans. She loved the arts and spent her off time running marathons. Blake glanced at her picture again. Her resemblance to Jacqueline was scary. Samantha had thought of everything; she'd even put the ladies' measurements and weights at the bottom of the page. In captions, Sam wrote a note about how dating services often use old Photoshopped high school pictures, but Alliance updated their photos every six months.

Candidate No. 2, Rita . . . Again, no last name. A physician's assistant taking classes for pre-med. She loved boating and spending time in exotic locations. She'd done her share of traveling, but Sam's papers didn't say how she afforded her hobby.

Candidate No. 3, Karen . . . Blake didn't bother looking for a last name. He knew it wouldn't be there. Karen should have been a model. Her stunning blue eyes and snow-blonde hair knocked a man's breath from his lungs. Karen wasn't in school and didn't have any student loans. She managed some type of nursing home and mentored kids at a boys and girls' club.

The women were perfect, so why did Blake have a sinking feeling that they were all wrong?

Blake pushed forward in his chair and picked up his phone. When his assistant picked up, Blake said, "Well, Mitch?"

"I still have a couple of calls unanswered, but I've found some interesting things about Miss Elliot."

"Great, bring them over."

Blake walked over to the floor-to-ceiling windows of his office and looked down at the city below. Running his shipping business from four points on the globe gave him the upper hand over his competitors. He'd built the business from a meager beginning, despite his father's disapproval. Blake's desire to prove to his father that he didn't need the man's money, or his title, fueled his drive. However, the Harrison name had opened many doors over the years, and pissing away the bulk of his inheritance wasn't something he was willing to do, especially since the old man was long dead.

Mitch knocked on the door to his office before he let himself in.

Turning on his heel, Blake nodded to the coffee table in the corner of his office where he could view the files Mitch had in his hand. "Let's do this over here."

Mitch sat and wasted little time spreading out papers for Blake to see.

"Samantha Elliot, twenty-seven years old, born in Connecticut to Harris and Martha Elliot."

Blake took his seat. "Why do those names sound familiar?"

"They should. Harris was center stage in the media several years back when he was charged with tax evasion and embezzlement. He and his family lived in a twenty-million-dollar mansion, with vacation homes in France and Hawaii—the whole big piece of the American pie."

Blake remembered it now. The big New York businessman had funneled his funds through glorified Ponzi schemes. He'd given out insurance policies for homes, land, business, and property to unsuspecting victims, with no intention of paying them off. If memory served him right, Blake recalled the feds having a hard time nailing him for corruption and instead managed to imprison him for not paying his taxes. His accounts and property were frozen, and his family fell apart.

"Martha, the wife, couldn't handle the drop in status, took a bottle of pills with a pint of gin, and never woke up." Mitch relayed the details of Samantha Elliot's family life as if it were a soap opera.

"According to the media, Samantha's sister, Jordan, tried to follow her mother's example, but failed and ended up with a lack of brain function. I'm still waiting on the details about where the girl is now. Samantha survived the ordeal, but ended up picking up the family pieces. She dropped out of college where she was studying business. She must have socked away a small amount of money the government didn't know about to take into her sister's care." Mitch took a breath and handed Blake a list of names.

"What's this?"

"These are people Miss Elliot has connections to. Growing up among the rich and connected resulted in some lasting friendships. The adults severed all ties to the Elliot family when they went down, but Samantha's friends didn't. There's a senator's daughter on that list and two rapidly progressing lawyers. I'm still not sure how she found out about your prior, but I have a call in back home."

Blake sifted through the papers and found a photo of the Elliot family during happy times. The small family stood aboard a yacht. Martha was pencil thin, and her daughters stood beside her in one-piece bathing suits. Samantha's hair was tied back in a ponytail, but it still had managed to blow into her face when the picture was taken. Jordan, much younger than Sam, had her mother's dark hair and tiny frame. Harris, a good fifty pounds overweight, rested a hand on his wife's shoulder and smiled for the camera.

Pictures were deceiving. His mind drifted to a similar family portrait of his. Blake's father stood behind his mother with a hand on her shoulder. His mother's white knuckles tensed on the armrest of the chair where she sat. Blake remembered the day the picture was taken. He and his father had argued about Blake taking a summer internship to better his college applications. Edmund refused to discuss Blake working for anyone, especially for free. Edmund believed an education was necessary for bragging to one's friends. Work, however, was a four-letter word—one no Harrison would touch so long as he had a say in their lives.

"I thought my family was dysfunctional," Blake whispered.

"I think Miss Elliot wins the prize."

Funny, Blake didn't think the prize was worth winning. "Where does Samantha live?"

"She rents a townhome in Tarzana."

"Roommates?"

"Hard to say."

Then, without knowing why he asked, he said, "Boyfriend?"

Mitch's eyes rounded to him. "I didn't look, but I will." Just then, the phone in Mitch's pocket rang.

He removed it and glanced at the number. "This is about the sister," he explained before he answered the call.

Mitch spoke into the line while Blake studied the names on the paper in his hand. Samantha had a lot of friends. He wondered if any of them helped her out financially.

Mitch made a whistling noise into the phone, grabbing Blake's attention.

"OK, thanks," Mitch said before he disconnected the call.

"What is it?"

"Miss Elliot truly needs your business."

"Really? Why?"

"Her sister is a patient of Moonlight Villas. Nice name for a fancy home for adults in her condition. The place racks up a six-figure bill every year."

Blake felt his eyes pinch together. "And no one is helping Miss Elliot with it?"

Mitch shook his head. "None that I've found. Her friends might give her advice, but there isn't a steady stream of money coming from anywhere but her business."

A business that Blake had already researched and knew all about.

"Interesting."

"So, what's she like?" It was the first personal question Mitch had asked.

Blake pictured her alabaster skin and the determined set of her jaw. And that voice. Damn, just thinking about it made him want to talk to her again.

"She's all business," Blake told his assistant. "You'd like her."

Being in control was her gig. So when Blake Harrison insisted on a dinner meeting to go over the prospective wife candidates, Samantha started working out potential scenarios.

Perhaps he'd recognized one of the women or placed a last name to a face. She purposely left off the surnames of the women so her male clients had to rate the merits of the women on their attributes, not their families. Sam knew all too well how people judged her by her parents' actions. After her parents' fall, she'd considered changing her name and even her hair color. She settled for moving to the West Coast and avoiding the media. The tabloid attention was short-lived. Once the newest scandal burst onto the scene, hers was forgotten. Living close to Hollywood constantly put the light on someone else. Her face hadn't been in the paper since her mother's funeral.

Maybe if Samantha had been a beauty and a media whore, the papers would have followed her. Dodging reporters proved easy when she'd started dressing like a wallflower.

So what did Harrison want to discuss? Maybe he'd already talked with his lawyer and needed details her papers hadn't covered. She'd thought of every conceivable loophole when she started her business. Her taxes were always paid—*Thank you, Dad*—and she always kept her contacts close to the chest. Nothing she'd ever done, in the way of background checks or private investigators, was illegal. The primary gender she turned to for information was female. Sam wasn't naive enough to believe that women weren't capable of illegal acts, but she had a hard time with trust and men. There weren't many in her life who hadn't let her down. In truth, she couldn't think of any.

The sun was still shining as she pulled her car into the parking lot of the most expensive beachfront restaurant in Malibu. Unable to avoid valet parking her car, Sam left her compact American-made sedan running as she stepped out of it. She thanked the attendant and watched him take the wheel, only to park it a few feet away. Her GMC looked completely out of place parked among all the Lexuses, Mercedeses, and Cadillacs.

Samantha stepped into the cool interior of the restaurant and let the mouthwatering smell of garlic and herbs wash over her senses. The last time she'd dined in a five-star restaurant was last year, with one of her happily married female clients. Sam had given up fine dining and opulent living long ago. Some things she missed. Eating something other than pop-in-the-microwave dinners and takeout was up there on her wish list.

Before Samantha had a chance to step up to the hostess, a man approached her. "Miss Elliot?"

Strange, he didn't seem to be wearing the required uniform of the staff. Maybe he was a manager.

"Yes?"

"Mr. Harrison is waiting for you."

Must be the manager. Samantha followed the well-dressed man deeper into the restaurant until he led her to a secluded booth with a full view of the Pacific. Blake Harrison saw her and stood as she approached.

Like before, his chiseled features and the way he filled out his designer suit brought a wave of awareness over her skin. He dominated the space by simply being there.

His eyes scanned her frame, and a small smile lifted the corner of his lips. She'd changed into a simple dress, not too casual, but certainly nothing fit for the Oscars. The expression on Blake's face said he approved. Not that she dressed to meet his approval, but she didn't want to appear out of place sitting beside him. She met his eyes and felt a hot current zip up her spine.

"You're late," he said, his voice teasing.

She opened her mouth, doing her best guppy impersonation, and then closed it. "Touché."

He smiled. "I took the liberty of ordering a bottle of wine. I hope you don't mind." Blake waited until she slid into the booth before reaching for the wine sitting in an ice bucket beside him.

She watched him pour the pale liquid into a stemmed glass and did her best not to stare. "Are we celebrating?"

"Perhaps," he said as he shifted the bottle over to his glass.

She wanted to rush and ask him which candidate he'd approved. Of course, he hadn't met the women yet, so she sincerely doubted he'd chosen one.

Blake lifted his glass and waited until she joined him in a toast. "To a successful business relationship."

A shiver of uncertainty flitted over her hand as she reached for her wine. The way Blake said *relationship* didn't sit well. After clicking her glass with his and sipping the wine, Samantha placed her hands in her lap to hide the slight tremor that would give away her feelings.

"I hope your drive wasn't awful."

OK, so they weren't going to start with business as she'd have liked. Instead of pushing him, she allowed the casual conversation to continue. "PCH is always *difficult* to traverse at dinnertime."

"Thank you for agreeing to meet me here."

"I'm surprised you picked this location. I'd think that a business dinner would be more appropriate in a less formal place." Less romantic, she wanted to add.

Blake relaxed into the booth. His sinfully handsome features made it nearly impossible to concentrate on the reason she was sitting across from him. It was entirely too easy to wade into his amazing gray eyes and fall into the warmth of his smile.

"It's against my nature to invite a beautiful woman to a bar for cocktails."

Oh boy, time to swing this train around. Samantha knew she wasn't beautiful—attractive, maybe—but the kind of beauty this man was drawn to was way out of Samantha's league. "You're charming, Mr. Harrison, but you're wasting it on me. I take it you've had an opportunity to look at the portfolios my assistant faxed over."

His eyes narrowed, but he didn't say a word. Samantha swallowed and clutched her hands together in her lap. Instead of avoiding his eyes, she met them head-on and kept her lips sealed.

It took a waiter stepping to the table to break the tension. The twentysomething server detailed the chef specials while Samantha picked up her menu. This was her client, and etiquette dictated that she be the one to pick up the bill, even if the restaurant was out of her budget. She settled on the swordfish and a small dinner salad and did her best to ignore the prices on the menu. She'd put it on her credit card and hope Mr. Harrison's check would clear before it came due.

When left alone, he asked, "Tell me, Samantha. Why would I be wasting my charm on you?"

He pronounced her name like a lover's caress,

smooth and silky. She heard a hint of an English accent. An accent she thought would be thick on his tongue because of his title.

"We're here to discuss your pending marriage to one of the three women from my service," she reminded him. "I'm not sure how charming *me* can work to any advantage for *you*."

"Does everything have to have an angle?"

"In business, yes." In her world, anyway.

"What about in your personal life?" He sat forward, his jacket opening as he did, and she noticed for the first time that he wasn't wearing a tie. His dress shirt's first two buttons were undone, and his bronze skin underneath caught her eye.

"We aren't here to discuss my personal life."

"I wouldn't be too sure about that. Your summary of my life this morning prompted me to do some digging of my own."

Samantha braced herself for his judgment. She never tried to hide her past but always stood a chance at losing a client because of the sins of her father. "One doesn't have to dig deep to unveil my past, Mr. Harrison."

"I thought we decided you'd call me Blake."

First names and talk of relationships. This was not going well. Samantha poured a little more wine down her throat, suddenly wishing it was something stronger. "My father is a horrible man. My mother was a coward. Neither of them reflects who I am or how I tend to my business, *Blake*."

"I didn't suggest otherwise."

She hated the defensive tone in her voice and the transient look of pity on Blake's face.

"You purposely left the last names of the women out. Why is that?"

Oh good, back to business. "I'm not the only one whose parents have darkened people's perceptions. I realize that family can pose a problem to any relationship, even if it's a business relationship. Starting out with information about the women themselves helps keep the door of possibilities open."

"Are the women all trust-fund babies or daughters of convicted felons?"

"Hardly. All three have severed their family ties—financially, anyway—which is why they're searching for security and not love."

Blake fingered the stem of his glass. She watched his movements and briefly wondered what it would feel like to have his hands on her skin, running up and down her arms, her thighs. Heat rushed up her neck, and she shifted her gaze away. "I can give you their names if you insist. If it's going to weigh on your decision, then it's best you know."

"That's not necessary. I've already picked the woman I'm going to offer a contract to."

Samantha's head shot in his direction right as the waiter brought their salads. She held her tongue while the waiter crushed fresh black pepper over their first course and topped off their glasses with the wine. The anticipation was eating her up. Whom had he picked and why? How could he actually decide to offer marriage to a person without even meeting her? That was extreme, even for the titled millionaire sitting across from her. Then again, maybe it wasn't. What did she really know about Blake Harrison? He liked his women busty, leggy, and lean. She hadn't found one picture of the man without a model type hanging from his arm. Hence the reason Samantha picked the three most beautiful women in her little black book—actually, her little black notebook. Still, how did a man pick from three pictures?

"Don't you want to meet them first?" Suddenly, the thought of him picking a wife from a photograph felt shallow, even to her. Were men so easily swayed by a beautiful face? The short answer was yes. She knew it was possible that Blake Harrison was as superficial as the next guy, but disappointment hovered over her as he proved it with his actions.

"The women in the pictures?"

Sam shook her head, confused. "Of course those women."

"No." He picked up his fork and took a bite.

No? Oh shit. He'd decided to marry someone else. The dollar signs she'd seen from the first mention of his name started to float out to sea.

"You've found someone else who has agreed to marry you?"

"She hasn't agreed—not yet, anyway." He took another bite, casual and in control.

If he wasn't going to use her service, then why the hell was she here? "So Alliance is a backup plan?" Maybe he wasn't kissing her off quite yet. Men like him didn't do things without reason.

"Not entirely."

Samantha dropped her fork and fixed him with a stare. "I'm sorry, Mr. Harrison, but I'm confused. Just this morning, you were looking for a contractual woman to meet your needs. Has something changed in the last few hours? Or are you unsatisfied with the ladies I presented?"

Blake gave up the pretense of eating and placed his hands on the table beside his plate. "The women you picked were perfect. Too perfect. My time frame to choose a wife is narrow. Getting to know each of those lovely ladies and making a decision is a luxury I don't have." He reached below the table and grasped a briefcase she hadn't seen. He removed a file folder and pushed it on the table in front of her.

"What's this?"

"The agreement my lawyer and I wrote up this afternoon."

She itched to open the folder, but laid her hand on it instead. "What agreement?"

Blake's gray eyes held onto hers. "I'm offering *you* a marriage contract."

Her heart fell in an audible thump. "I'm not on the menu, Mr. Harrison." She pushed the papers back toward him. He caught her hand under his and held it firmly. The contact shot that sizzle she'd felt when she'd first seen him straight to her toes and back up again. The constant thud of her heart started to rise, and gooseflesh spread over her bare arms. Sam's entire body tingled, and the only part of them touching was their hands.

"Everyone has a price, Samantha."

"Not me." She tried to pull away, but he squeezed her fingers to keep her from running.

"I'm setting up a trust fund to take care of Jordan for life. Even if something were to happen to you, Jordan would be taken care of."

Sam's mouth opened with that guppy look again. A bomb going off couldn't have shocked her more. Blake had done his homework, knew of her sister and her needs. "My sister is only twenty-two years old. She could live to be a hundred." Not likely, according to the doctors, but there wasn't proof she'd die young, either.

"And her care costs you a hundred and six thousand a year. Those expenses will only go up." His hand loosened on hers, but she didn't pull away.

"You're willing to pay me over eight million dollars to be your wife for a year?"

"Plus twenty percent. That is your fee, right?"

Samantha nodded slowly, then shook her head. "Why me?"

"Why *not* you?" His thumb started to move over her hand, but she was still too stunned to move.

"I'm not your type."

"My type?"

"Tall, blonde, and gorgeous."

He chuckled, and the laugh grounded her. This was a business deal, after all, nothing more, nothing less. Blake had turned her hand over and was rubbing the inside of her wrist with soothing circles. OK, maybe a marriage contract was a bit more than a business deal.

She removed her hand from under his. "What would marriage to you look like?"

"Your life wouldn't have to change," he said as he lifted his wine to his lips. "A quick trip to the justice of the peace, maybe Vegas. We'd have to make a few appearances over the first few months to satisfy the lawyers my father hired before his death and my cousin who stands to gain should this not work out. I spend half of my time in Europe, half here in Malibu. So we wouldn't cramp each other's daily life."

"Why not find a wife in Europe?"

"To minimize the relentless media eyes in Europe. The US doesn't have tabloids dedicated to kings and queens, dukes and duchesses. The newness of my nuptials will wear off quickly here."

The stipulations in his father's will stated that Blake had to be married and settled by his thirty-sixth birthday in order to inherit the late duke's wealth and keep his title. After much debate, the lawyers determined that after a year of marriage, the estate would relinquish his inheritance and lift any further legal restrictions. This was what Samantha's contacts in London had told her.

"What kind of appearances?"

"A small reception and a few appearances in public venues. I'd need you to come with me to London to sign papers with the lawyers in regard to my title—*our* titles."

She swallowed. She'd forgotten about the whole duchess thing. "I've no idea what being a duchess is about."

Blake lifted his fork and started eating again. "I've never had one, so I'm not completely sure, either."

Samantha couldn't help but offer a laugh. "This is crazy."

"I'm surprised you think so. The arrangement makes perfect sense to me."

The waiter returned with their meals and quickly left.

Samantha remembered the advice she'd given Blake earlier in the day. *It will be up to you to keep it in your pants, Mr. Harrison.* Perhaps he'd picked her because it would be easy to stay out of her bed. That made perfect sense. Maybe he'd seen the pictures of the women she'd picked out and found them perfectly doable.

"What's the matter?" he asked.

She really needed to work on her poker face. "Nothing. I . . . This is a lot to think about. I wasn't expecting this proposal."

"But you're considering it."

"I'd be a fool not to."

"You don't strike me as foolish." He took a bite of his prime rib with a gleam in his eye.

No, she wasn't a fool. "I'll look over your contract tomorrow."

"Excellent."

Chapter Three

The plane reached cruising altitude, and the pilot told them they could remove their seat belts for the forty-five-minute flight to Las Vegas. Samantha had said very little once they'd boarded.

After she'd agreed to be his wife for a year, Blake solidified his plans for a wedding chapel visit in Sin City. He believed a seemingly romantic wedding in Vegas would appear more legitimate to Parker and Parker than a drive to city hall.

Blake released his seat belt and took advantage of the freedom. He moved about the cabin of his private jet to open a bottle of champagne. When he glanced at his fiancée, he noted how her hands twisted in her lap. Funny, he was the one with everything to lose, but she was the one fidgeting. "Here, maybe this will help." He handed her a tall flute and sat across from her in the oversize plush leather chair.

"Am I so obvious?"

"The white knuckles give you away."

Samantha swallowed half the champagne in one gulp. "I never wanted to be an actress."

"I'd bet the studios would pay top dollar for you to do voice-overs."

She shrugged. "If I had a dollar for every time I've heard that."

He could only imagine. "You do have an amazing voice."

Samantha's eyes scurried away from his, and her cheeks started to take on a rosy glow. "I think this marriage thing will work out better if we don't find anything about each other *amazing*. Nothing personal, anyway."

"You're probably right, but being honest is some-thing we both agreed to. And your voice is sexy as hell." Watching her squirm under his compliment was worth him showing his cards. She wore a full-on blush now, and it was nothing short of adorable.

Just like that, her glass was empty again. "I'm not sure if I should thank you or encourage you to be less shallow."

"Ouch."

"You wanted honesty."

He watched her toe off her high heels and tuck her legs under the seat. Some of the color started to return to her fingers. Obviously, dissing him put her at ease. He wasn't sure how to take that. "The only person in my life who's called me shallow is Carter."

"Your best friend?"

"My one *real* friend."

"Really? I'd think a man with your wealth would have an entourage of friends."

"Money brings people, not friends," he said.

"Amen to that. I take it Carter knows about us. Our arrangement, I mean."

"He does."

"What about your girlfriends? Do they know?"

Now it was his turn to squirm. Even though their marriage would be a sham, talking about his lovers with his wife didn't feel right.

"Telling my girlfriends, as you call them, would be equivalent to calling the *Inquisitor* and giving them a full-page interview." Blake finished his wine and stood to refill their glasses.

"You don't trust them?"

"Not with this."

"How do men do it?"

"Do what?"

"Sleep with women they don't trust?" Samantha thanked him for the wine and sipped it slowly this time.

"It's called attraction."

Laughing, she said, "It's called lust."

"That too." Blake's insides started to warm. When was the last time he'd held a conversation with a woman about the motivations of men? Never. He found he liked it.

"So, what did you say to your . . . What do you call the women in your life? Lovers?"

The title of lover started to feel too personal. "I haven't told them anything, yet."

She lifted her manicured eyebrows high. "I'd like to be a fly on the wall during those conversations. *Oh, darling, by the way, I got married over the weekend.*" Samantha laughed at her own joke.

"I don't think I'll tell them like that." He wasn't sure how he would break the news and honestly hadn't given it a second thought.

"You do realize you stand the risk of losing them both, right?"

"How did you know there were two?" He shook his head and put a hand in the air. "Never mind. I forgot about your intensive background check. You don't have to worry about either of them. You'll never meet."

Samantha placed a hand over her chest and smiled. "Shallow and a tiny bit naive."

Lord, there she went calling him names again. "Excuse me?"

"If you and I were dating and you suddenly up and married another woman, as much as I'd hate myself for doing it, I'd figure out a way to meet the woman I didn't measure up to. Women are emotional creatures, Mr. Har . . . Blake. I might fight that gender trait with a nine iron, but I still can't beat down certain impulses. I highly doubt Vanessa and Jackie—"

"Jacqueline," he corrected.

"Excuse me, *Jacqueline* are any different. Which one is most likely to be heartbroken?"

The honesty thing was going too far. Even if the casual trek through his personal life lifted the edge of unease from his fiancée's frame, he wasn't comfortable. Samantha had tucked her feet under her bottom, and for the first time since they'd met, she was relaxed. The smile on her face didn't look forced, and her green eyes glistened with a spark of mischief. He would have liked to put her in this mood by doing something other than discussing his previous lovers, and previous was what they were. He thought for a moment about what Vanessa and Jacqueline would say once they heard of his marriage. Vanessa would be prone to slapping him and walking away. Jacqueline wouldn't be as dramatic, but continuing his relationship with her would be risky. "Both women knew about the other."

"But which one wanted more?"

"I can't believe my fiancée is asking me these questions."

"Which one, Blake?"

Samantha was relentless.

"Vanessa. Though, I doubt she'd seek you out. Besides, she lives in London and only visits New York for short periods of time."

"Right, and Jacqueline lives between New York and Spain."

The pilot's voice sounded over the loudspeaker, announcing their approach to the Nevada airport. "You've done your homework." Blake moved to the seat beside her.

"Always." She looked proud of herself.

"You'll inform me if either of them end up on your doorstep?"

Samantha straightened her legs and clicked her seat belt. "You'll be the first to know."

47

The jet started to descend, and Samantha glanced out the window. Between the wine and the conversation, she no longer looked like she'd run from the altar. Blake took her hand in his and felt her jump. "You might try to control that," he suggested.

She glanced at their hands and took a deep breath. "I'm trying."

Blake left his hand on hers and made a mental note to hold it often. Did she jump because his touch bothered her or because she liked it? Maybe she liked it and that bothered her. Oh well, he mused, she'd have to grow used to it.

As the plane descended from the sky, the wheels skidded on the runway, and Blake watched a play of emotions cross over Samantha's face. Her pouty pink lips that had been smiling only moments before were now drawn into a straight line. With any other woman, he would have leaned over and kissed the worry away. The unexpected desire to do just that welled up inside him. How would she taste? Sweet from the wine, he decided. The thought of her sexy voice whispering into his ear, encouraging him to do more than kiss her, surged to his groin. He forced his gaze away from her face and squeezed her hand.

When the pilot announced they were clear to unbuckle, Blake turned to Samantha. "Ready to get married?"

She turned her hand over and laced her fingers

with his. "What the hell. I didn't have anything better planned for today."

Blake tossed his head back and laughed.

After a short limo ride to the newest resort hotel on the strip, Samantha stood at the altar holding Blake's hand. During the ceremony, she gave him the ring he'd provided to give to him, but she gasped when he slid a four-carat diamond-encrusted sapphire on her finger. "For my duchess," he said. Even the minister gaped at the ring.

Somewhere between the limo and the ring, Samantha realized that Blake would likely kiss her at the completion of the ceremony. Why wouldn't he? If the lawyers questioned the minister and the witness, Blake would want them to believe that they were madly in love and had eloped. So, instead of considering her marriage vows, vows neither of them planned to keep, Sam couldn't stop thinking about the impending kiss.

The room started to feel too warm, and her palms started to sweat. She repeated her vows and listened to Blake promise to forsake all others.

". . . I now pronounce you husband and wife. You may kiss your bride."

She gulped.

Although she was ready to fall into a heap on the floor, Blake was a statue of control. He wrapped one arm around her waist and dropped his gaze to hers. His gray eyes sparkled, and his perfect lips pulled up at the corners.

She licked her lips and forced them into a smile. Her stomach twisted as he drew her closer. Blake used his free hand to hold her cheek. He hesitated over her lips. Samantha felt the heat of his breath and let her body relax into his embrace.

Then his lips were there, moist, firm, and completely intoxicating. Electricity zapped her brain and wiggled down her body. Even in heels, she tiptoed up to meet his kiss. His arm crushed her body to his. Her breasts pushed against his taut chest. She gasped and his tongue slid inside her mouth.

Samantha forgot about the minister, about the strangers watching, and simply gave in to the pleasure Blake Harrison evoked inside her body. It had been eons since she'd been kissed, and certainly none had compared to this kiss. Maybe it was the fact that she was learning Blake's touch after exchanging wedding vows, or maybe it was the man himself. Perhaps all dukes kissed like he did.

Someone cleared his throat, and Samantha felt Blake pull away. Something close to confusion settled in his eyes. Was it possible that Blake felt that kiss as deeply as she did? She thought of the two women he'd have to explain to and decided the kiss couldn't have affected him nearly as much as it had her. Blake, her husband, was a player. She'd have to remember that.

"Congratulations, Mr. and Mrs. Harrison. If you'll follow me and sign a couple of papers, the two of you can begin your honeymoon." The minister ushered them from the small chapel to an office where Samantha signed her name next to Blake's on the official certificate.

Just like that, she was a married woman.

Blake wasn't sure how he'd envisioned his wedding night, but the previous night hadn't been it. He'd secured a honeymoon suite at a luxurious resort and casino and slept on the couch, all the while listening to his wife mill about the bedroom until she finally settled sometime around one in the morning.

Their kiss had unsettled him. It started out as an act, a public display of affection that, if needed, could be reported back to the lawyers. But ever since he and Samantha left the chapel, the performance was something he'd wanted to repeat. The way her face lit up, and her inability to meet his eye, proved she was as turned on as he. Dammit, he shouldn't be lusting over his wife. A wife of convenience. A wife who often put a smile on his face and made him question his playboy ways and superficial pastimes.

He remembered her warning about "keeping it in his pants," or something to that effect. He needed to get far away from Mrs. Harrison soon, or keeping it in his pants would be impossible.

Blake tucked away the blanket and pillow he'd used the night before and waited for the light in Samantha's room to filter in enough to wake her up. He'd already sent notice to the offices in London about his "whirlwind" wedding to his "love at first sight" bride. It wouldn't take long for word to spread. Chances were, he'd have to retrieve his wife within a couple of weeks to convince those who watched that their nuptials were heartfelt. He'd use those few weeks to build a few fences around his libido. He didn't worry about his heart, but if he screwed up Samantha's, he risked losing everything. That risk was entirely too high.

A soft knock on the door alerted him that room service had arrived.

Blake opened the door and directed the uniformed staff to wheel the cart into the center of the room. The rich smell of coffee piqued his senses and made his mouth water. As the waiter handed him the bill, the door from the bedroom opened and out walked the smoky-eyed, sleepy vision of his wife wrapped in a fluffy white bathrobe.

"Is that coffee I smell?" Samantha's bedroom voice ripped through him and he groaned. Even the kid shuffling the room service tray forgot what he was doing as he turned toward the voice.

"I ordered breakfast."

"Oh, good, I'm starving." Sam's bare feet

pattered closer. Her petite legs flashed through the slit in the robe.

The waiter dropped the bill, and Blake moved to block Samantha from view. The kid turned red as he picked up the bill and handed it over. Blake quickly signed it and hustled the kid out of the room.

He took a deep breath and stiffened his spine before he turned around. His bravado didn't work. The hair on the back of Blake's neck stood on end. Samantha was peeking under the silver lids with one hand and pushing her rumpled hair back with the other. She was sexy as sin.

She lifted the coffee and started to pour. "How do you like it?"

Blake closed his eyes and forced his naked thoughts out of his lust-filled mind. "Black."

He crossed to the table and sat.

Working quietly, Samantha handed him a cup before she sprinkled a little sugar in her coffee.

As the first sip met her lips, she sunk into her chair with a sigh. The sound was throaty and brought another wave of awareness over his skin. He needed to get the hell out of Vegas, or all bets for not bedding his wife were off.

Not realizing the effect she was having on him, Samantha lifted her legs and sat them on the opposite chair. The robe gapped open, revealing another flash of thigh.

Blake's body responded with a vengeance. His

hardened length pushed to painful levels, forcing him to shift in his chair to avoid Samantha's notice.

"How did you sleep?" she asked, not bothering to cover her alabaster skin.

"OK," he lied, trying hard to divert his eyes from her thighs.

"Really? I tossed and turned. I'm more keyed up about this marriage than I thought I would be."

How difficult would it be to tell her he felt the same? But then, that would sound as if he weren't in control. Blake had to have an iron fist on everything in his life, including his marriage.

"I'm sure you'll get used to it, especially after I leave for London."

She reached forward and removed a piece of toast from the plate. "When are you leaving?"

"Tomorrow."

"Tomorrow?" She sounded surprised.

"I'll take you back to LA and introduce you to my staff and Carter before I prepare to leave."

She nibbled on her bread. "Won't that look suspicious, you leaving so soon after our marriage?"

"It might, so we'll have to make things look good. Daily phone calls, something that proves we're talking to each other. My father's lawyers are merciless. They hired private eyes on behalf of my father when I was in college to report back about my transgressions."

"Isn't that extreme?"

"My father offered kickbacks—lucrative kickbacks—for every offense they found. I doubt anything has changed since his death." Because Blake didn't want to dive into more family history quite yet, he asked, "Do you have a passport?"

"Not since I was twenty and the Feds took it. There shouldn't be a problem with me obtaining one. In any event, it will be a good excuse to explain why I'm not going with you."

She was smiling now, waking up as she finished her first cup of coffee. He didn't think his switch of subjects went unnoticed, but she kept any questions she had to herself.

"I'll start the paperwork on Monday."

"Sounds good."

"I was thinking, last night when I couldn't sleep, if I should change my name or not. A lot of women keep their names even after they marry. It might be easier." She sat forward and dished up some scrambled eggs.

He didn't like the sound of that and would question why later. "If we had married for love, and not for convenience, would you have taken my name?"

"But we didn't."

"But what if we had?"

She glanced down at the family ring he'd placed on her finger the day before. "Yes, I probably would have."

He finished his coffee with a smug sense of satisfaction. "Then you change your name. I don't want anyone questioning anything. We'll have enough obstacles to overcome with you and I living the majority of this year on different continents."

She looked like she wanted to argue but sighed instead. "You're probably right."

"I'm going to set up an account for you before I leave and give you the keys to my house." The thought of her walking around his house in a fuzzy white robe brought a smile to his face.

"That isn't necessary."

"I disagree," he said, dishing up his own eggs, sausage, and toast. "I wouldn't leave a wife without resources."

"Fine, but I won't use them. I don't need your money, at least not now that you've taken care of Jordan. And I have my own place." She chewed her food slowly before swallowing.

"I still owe you your twenty percent. Use the account, Samantha. My wife wouldn't go without, and I won't have people saying I'm not taking care of you."

She dropped her hand to the table. "I won't ruin your image, Blake."

"You will if you're driving an old car and skimping on personal items. I'm not suggesting you buy a yacht, just don't shop at the big-box stores." He pictured the media catching her in Walmart and cringed.

"You realize how snobby that sounds, right?"

"I don't care. My girlfriends shopped at designer stores; therefore, my wife won't be taking dresses off the sale rack." Blake noticed her jaw tighten and prepared himself for an argument.

"Is there something wrong with how I dress?"

Oh boy . . . He was walking in a minefield without a lead jacket. "I didn't say that."

"Oh, yes, you did."

He stopped eating. "You know I'm right about this."

Her lips twitched, but she didn't deny him. "Fine."

"Good." *I won.* Lord, when was the last time he'd argued with a woman about not wanting to spend his money? He found a smile forming on his lips.

"What's so funny?" Her eyes were sparkling with unreleased fury. They were drop dead gorgeous.

"I think we just had our first marital spat."

Her shoulders slumped and folded in with laughter. "I guess we did."

"And I won," he pointed out.

Samantha fixed him with a heated stare. "Don't expect that to continue."

No, he mused, he wasn't delusional enough to think he'd win every time. However, winning the first placed a certain amount of whipped cream on top of his marital pie.

Chapter Four

Twenty-six hours after they'd said *I do,* the media discovered Samantha and Blake as they disembarked from Blake's jet. Thank God she'd had the foresight to bring large-framed sunglasses to hide the stress in her eyes. The media hadn't changed since her father's arrest. They blocked their way, snapped pictures, and asked questions.

Blake kept a possessive arm around her waist as he ushered her from the airport. With any luck, someone in Hollywood would fall off the wagon and remove the spotlight by the end of the weekend. Otherwise, she'd be dealing with the paparazzi alone.

Blake called out little things as they passed, words like *the love of my life* and *she knocked my socks off.* He sounded so sincere. If she wasn't in on his ploy, even she would have believed him. At one point, Blake dipped his lips to her ear and whispered, "It will be worse in Europe, so take hold of your inner snob and smile."

She laughed and leaned against him to make her way around a car door. The photo snapped at that moment made it on all of the major television channels and into three tabloid magazines.

Blake's friend, Carter, turned out to be a surprise. His blond hair and surfer good looks were opposite those of her husband's. Turned out, he was smart, pragmatic, and had a killer sense of humor. He'd given Sam his cell phone number and encouraged her to use it if she needed anything while Blake was out of town.

As mapped out, Blake gave Samantha access to his home sitting high above Malibu with a beautiful ocean view. The estate was huge—ten thousand square feet on ten acres. His staff included a cook, a maid, and a grounds crew. Neil, Blake's driver, watched over the staff and lived in a guest cottage. The size of the man would intimidate a football team. Blake made it clear that he doubled as a bodyguard.

Once she'd wished her husband a safe flight, Samantha found herself back in her rented townhome, deep in thought. Blake's assessment and execution of taking a wife had been an extremely smart move. Even a strong woman like herself turned her head at his kind of wealth. She twisted the ring on her finger and admired it. "I don't even want to know what you cost," she murmured to her hand. She'd have to return it in fifty-four weeks, but she'd enjoy it until then.

The door to her townhome slammed after she heard Eliza yell, "No comment."

"Holy shit, how long are we going to have to put up with that?" More friend than employee, Eliza swung her purse off her arm and tossed it on the coffee table.

"They'll go away in a day or two."

"You sound so sure."

"Been there, done that. Our divorce will bring out even more media."

Eliza tossed a paper on the table. It opened to the now-familiar photograph of Sam and Blake laughing. "You two are very convincing."

Samantha smiled. Despite her desire for the media to disappear, she liked the pictures they'd taken. After all, they were her wedding photos. "We don't look half bad together."

"Half bad? You guys look happy as larks."

"Do larks look happy?" Sam teased.

"I've no idea. I'm sorry I didn't meet him when he dropped you off." Eliza flopped onto the couch and tossed her long legs up on the coffee table.

"He didn't. Actually, his driver did."

"Driver?" Eliza had the most amazing chocolate-brown eyes that shot wide-open with her question.

"He's rich. Why on earth would he drive himself?" Samantha laughed and rolled her eyes, doing her best snob impersonation.

"Well, la-di-da. Excuse me." But her friend was laughing.

The business phone rang, and Eliza jumped from the couch to answer it. "Alliance."

Samantha lent half an ear while Eliza listened to the person on the line.

Even with him towering over her vertically

challenged frame, the picture of her and Blake wasn't that bad.

"We don't have any comments at this time," Eliza was saying. "No, we're not an escort service . . . Again, no comment." With a frustrated sigh, she hung up.

"I should have seen that coming." The media would tear up her business if given a chance.

"We should probably have a standard statement to give them."

"Good idea. I'll draft something and run it past Blake."

The phone rang again with another reporter asking questions. Within half an hour, Sam and Eliza gave up and unplugged the business line. With any luck, the hype would blow over soon. The publicity could bring in new clients, so long as Samantha could maintain their anonymity. With every entertainment press sitting on her doorstep, that couldn't happen, so she'd have to put off new customers for a while.

"This is crazy," Eliza said as she flicked the shades from the living room closed. A few paparazzi had camped out on the street and managed to swing their lenses around every time either one of them popped open the blinds.

"I'll make us some dinner. You don't mind staying tonight, do you?" Eliza had lived in the spare room up until she moved in with her current boyfriend six months ago.

"Is that your way of asking me to stay?"

"Hell yeah. I don't want to be alone with them outside. They'll just follow you home anyway," Sam told her.

"Fine, but I get to pick the movie. Tell me you have wine."

"Don't I always?" Samantha turned off the lights on her porch and fastened the dead bolt on the front door. The two of them dressed down into sweats and comfortable T-shirts and settled in front of the television with slices of cheap pizza and a nice bottle of merlot.

"I have a feeling we won't be doing this much more," Eliza said between bites.

"Why's that?" Sam was writing a few notes in her notebook, trying to work a press release.

"You're a married woman."

"So?" They both knew it was in name only. Right now, Blake was probably asleep in the bedroom on his private plane and not giving her a second thought.

"You're married to a duke, Sam. Do you have any idea how huge that is?"

"It's just a title. Like 'sir' or 'doctor.' Only, Blake didn't have to work to obtain it."

"He inherited the title automatically when his father died, right?" Eliza had shifted her feet under her butt and placed a bowl of popcorn between them on the couch.

Samantha nodded.

"But he needed to get married to inherit the estate?"

"In most cases, the title and the estate go together to the first male born to the duke and duchess. But Blake's father was a Class A jerk. He stipulated in his will that his estate was to be divided up, dissolved for all intents and purposes, if Blake didn't settle down by his thirty-sixth birthday. One cousin would get a portion of the estate, a small allowance would go to Blake's mother and sister, and the rest goes to charity."

"That's cold. The dad didn't make it so his own wife could stay in the home she'd made hers for years?"

"I guess not."

Eliza sat forward. "What an ass."

"Blake told me that a title without the estate is like a king without a country. The royalty thing boggles my mind."

Samantha's cell phone buzzed beside her. Blake's name popped up on the screen. A wave of excitement rode up her back. "Hey," she answered.

"I wanted to reach you before you went to bed." He sounded tired, and the background noise made it difficult for her to hear him.

"And I thought you'd be at twenty thousand feet. Where are you?"

"I was delayed in New York. I'll be leaving here within the hour." Their day had started out early, and it seemed his wasn't going to end anytime soon. Samantha actually felt sorry for him.

"Listen, the media is nuts here. I thought we should give a press release sooner than later. Maybe get them off my back," Samantha suggested.

"Are you OK? They aren't harassing you, are they?" Worry etched his voice.

"No, I'm—"

"I wish you'd stay at my house."

"We've gone over this. I'm fine here. People will buy a slow turnover in my life." She heard a PA announcing flights. "How does this sound? Mr. and Mrs. Harrison would like you to respect their privacy while they adjust to their rapidly changing lives. Their courtship and subsequent wedding was as unexpected to them as it has been to the world. A pending reception is being planned to introduce the couple and reveal details of their love match."

"Love match?" It was the only thing Blake questioned.

"That does sound hokey. I'll think of something else."

Blake laughed. "The only other thing you need to change is our names."

"What?"

His voice was cutting out.

"Yeah, it needs to read Lord and Lady Harrison, the Duke and Duchess of Albany. Listen, I've got to go. I'll call in the morning. Call Carter or Neil if you need anything." Then the line went dead.

A shiver of dread fell on her like a curtain falling on a stage. "Oh. My. God."

"What?" Eliza stopped shoveling popcorn in her mouth and stared at Samantha with wide eyes.

"I'm in over my head." Duchess! She truly was a duchess. The weight of the title choked out all other thoughts.

"You haven't used the credit cards." Those were the first words out of Blake's mouth three days later.

Samantha was jogging on the beach with a Bluetooth snug in her ear. The media had lightened up at the front door, but the calls kept coming. She decided to give Eliza some much-deserved time off and escaped her town house as often as possible.

"Hello to you too." She slowed her pace so she could manage a conversation.

"You sound out of breath. What are you doing?"

"Jogging."

"Oh." He sounded surprised. "What's that noise?"

"The wind. I'm at the beach." She dodged a few rocks and continued her run.

"Is that safe? Is someone with you?"

She laughed. "Yes, it's safe, Detective Dan, and no, no one is with me." Although she teased him, she enjoyed his concern. Sam couldn't remember a time when someone cared if she jogged alone.

"I'm sure you didn't call for details about my exercise routine. What's up?"

"I wanted to make sure you had filled out the forms for your passport."

"Spent six hours at the social security office on Tuesday. Name change, passport, the whole deal. I asked them to rush, but they said it would take a minimum of ten business days."

The cool morning air and fog wet the edges of her hair and plastered it to her face as she ran. She loved this time of day. The beach had a smattering of joggers and a dozen surfers at the point. She made it to the beach at least once a week to run. At other times, she took a neighborhood route. Admittedly, the blocks where she usually jogged were becoming more and more questionable, and Samantha opted to drive to a safer trail or park. She couldn't help wondering how the beach by Blake's home would compare.

"Ten days isn't going to work. I'll put a call in and get it faster."

"The rush I paid for took it from a month to ten days. They said I couldn't get it any faster." Her breath came in heated pants, but she kept moving.

"I'll take care of it." His take-charge attitude struck her as funny.

"Does anyone ever deny the great and powerful Blake Harrison?" she teased.

"Only you. Why aren't you out shopping? I

told you to indulge." He wasn't happy about something. She could hear it in his voice.

"Let me guess. You saw a tabloid picture of me in an old shirt and jeans."

He hesitated.

"That's it, isn't it?" She started laughing and had to stop running to catch her breath. "Oh, Blake, let it go."

"Go shopping, Samantha. Our reception is going to bring out dignitaries and several influential families. We'll be attending the theater, polo matches, you name it."

"My cutoffs aren't going to work?" Tears stung her eyes.

"Even I saw *Pretty Woman*. Go shopping!"

The thought of him enduring a chick flick brought on more laughter. "I hope the woman was worth it."

"What woman?"

"The one who dragged you to the cinema."

He laughed. The sound filled her head with pictures of his handsome face and gray eyes. "It was my sister."

"That explains it."

"She won a bet. I had to take her or lose her respect." His voice eased as the conversation continued. Seemed it always did after a few minutes on the phone. Sam found herself looking forward to his calls. "Did you stop running?" he asked.

Samantha glanced down the deserted beach and

placed a hand on her hip. "Yeah," she said, as her breath hissed.

Blake groaned.

"What is it?"

"You want an honest answer?"

"Always." She turned to the breeze and forced her breath to slow down.

"Between the heavy breathing and that voice of yours, I'm having a hard time sitting still."

Her heart gave a hard kick in her chest. She sucked in her lower lip. "Well then, I won't describe what I'm wearing or how I look and ruin your fantasy."

He chuckled. "I'm sure the paparazzi are there somewhere and a picture will be on my desk in the morning."

Sam glanced around but didn't see anyone with a camera. "Maybe."

"Before I go, I tried calling your house, but the phone line was out of order."

"The line developed static. The repair guys are coming in the morning to fix it. I've added caller ID so I can screen the media." Sam pivoted and started a slow jog back to her car.

"Solid plan. I'll call tomorrow."

She smiled and just for fun added, "Oh, and Blake?"

"Yeah."

She dipped her voice even lower and breathed into the phone. "I'm all hot and sweaty too."

"Errrr." His groan vibrated her earpiece.

After he hung up, Samantha questioned the wisdom of flirting. As the smile threatened to leave permanent dimples on her cheeks, she shoved her concerns away and simply enjoyed the thought of a man showing interest in her as a woman.

Even if that man was her husband.

The media must have given up, she thought as she walked up the steps to her townhome. There weren't camera-holding fortysomething-year-olds ducking behind bushes or zooming in from the corner. She stepped into her house, tossed her keys on the entryway table, and started for the stairs.

When the doorbell rang, she twisted around and opened it on impulse. Midswing, she realized she was probably inviting an undesired picture, one that would have Blake shaking his head tomorrow.

But the person beyond the door wasn't a reporter or a photographer in pursuit of a quick buck.

It was worse. Vanessa.

The woman staring back at her was everything Samantha was not. She had blonde hair so pure it couldn't possibly come from a bottle, high cheekbones, and brilliant blue eyes. Long legs peeked out from beneath a tailored silk skirt that never hung from a rack in a department store.

Well, Blake had good taste in women, she'd give him that.

"You know who I am." Vanessa van Buren was not the jilted lover Samantha would have pegged to show up unannounced. To peek from afar, maybe, but to knock on her door took some guts. The boisterous Jacqueline would have been more Sam's bet.

She was wrong.

"And you know who I am."

Vanessa's gaze swept up and down Sam's frame, and a smirk skimmed her lips. Vanessa was dressed in Gucci, Samantha in Target. There was a time when Samantha was younger, before the fall of her father, that a friend had given her a piece of friendly advice. She'd said, "Don't go into battle without a full arsenal." Samantha and a high school rival were both trying to capture the attention of a boy at the time. From that day forward, Samantha never left home without a full face of makeup and a designer label on her back.

She glanced down at her cotton shorts and T-shirt that read JOGGERS KEEP THE PACE and cringed.

"Are you going to invite me in?"

That's sooo not going to happen. "I don't see the purpose."

Vanessa stepped forward and pushed her way in anyway. Samantha considered stopping her but would have had to physically restrain her. That picture in the morning tabloid probably wouldn't bode well for Blake or Samantha.

Samantha shut the door and kept Vanessa from

walking farther into the room. "That's far enough."

"This won't take long." Vanessa's voice held tightly controlled anger as her eyes kept a constant surveillance of the room. "What could Blake possibly see in you?"

Sam crossed her arms over her chest. "Are your claws always out? Or do you put them away at night?"

"Clever. Do you know I slept with him just two weeks ago?"

Several retorts came to her lips, but Sam squelched them. "Blake and I never wanted to hurt anyone." Sam did her level best to avoid the image of the two of them doing the naked tango.

"Blake hurts everyone . . . eventually. You'll discover that soon enough."

"I really think you should leave." Samantha was ready to stop playing nice. This wasn't a woman who was in love with a man. This was a snake coiling for a strike.

"Does he know about your father? About the sordid family you've hidden in your past?"

Samantha's jaw tightened, and her nails dug into her arms. "Blake knows everything."

The cold, calculated stare in Vanessa's eyes held a hint of knowledge. "Everything? Are you sure about that?"

She had nothing to hide—well, almost nothing to hide. Samantha's sins were buried so deep not even her connections could find them. "You sound like a desperate woman, Vanessa. I have to tell you, it doesn't look good."

The smirk on the other woman's face fell. "There is nothing about me screaming desperation. You, on the other hand, are a poster child for the word."

"Ding, ding. This round's officially over." Samantha opened the door wide, not caring who snapped the shot. "Move it, or I'll be forced to shove my Nikes up your Pradas."

Her rapid heartbeat was aching to do some serious kicking.

"Careful, you don't know who you're dealing with."

Samantha shoved her frame as close to Vanessa as she could without touching her. "Lady, you've no idea *what* I'm capable of. To think, when Blake told me about you, I actually felt sorry for you. What a waste. I'm not sure what he was thinking."

Venom spiked from the other woman's eyes. Turning on her heel, Vanessa slid on dark glasses and marched to a red sports car parked on the street.

Slamming the door would have proven how far the catty woman had dug herself under Samantha's skin. Instead, she closed it and slumped against the frame. Her hands started to tremble as the force of the encounter raced through her bloodstream.

The sound of gravel being kicked up from a car met her ears. "That was pleasant." Sam pushed away from the door and reached for her purse.

Not wanting to talk, she opened up her text messaging and pressed Blake's cell number.

Do I win a prize for being right? she texted her husband.

While waiting for his reply, she locked the door and made her way up the stairs to the shower.

Her phone buzzed on the top step.

Right about what?

Just met your blonde viper. Not sure what you saw in her past the obvious. And because she really didn't trust herself to speak, she added, *Getting in the shower, talk later.*

Sam tossed her phone on her bed and strode to the bathroom. Her nerves started to settle slowly. She glanced at her reflection in the mirror. The morning mist played havoc with her hair. Her face held a hint of chapped red on her cheeks. "What a mess."

In the other room, her phone rang.

She ignored it.

Samantha tugged her shirt from her body and tossed it in the hamper. Her high school friend's words rang in her ears. *Full arsenal.*

"You know something, Blake? I think I'll take you up on your open credit card." With women like Vanessa showing up, she might as well suit up for battle. Having been born with a proverbial silver spoon in her mouth, she knew how to play. She'd just chosen not to.

Until now.

Chapter Five

B lake rubbed his hands over his face for the umpteenth time that day. Samantha's text message shook him, and then he hadn't been able to speak with her since.

What the hell was Vanessa thinking? What did she say to his wife? Married less than a week and already Blake found himself trying to find ways of keeping his lover and wife separate. Blake hadn't even spoken with Vanessa since he put the ring on Samantha's finger. He'd tried to call her once. But when her housekeeper said she wasn't taking his calls, he didn't think they had anything more to say to each other.

Jacqueline had sent him a cold "call when you're tired of her" retort.

What did the word *viper* mean? It couldn't be good.

Dammit. If it would take something other than a full-day flight, he'd be on his plane now. Making rash decisions wasn't his style. His plan was to return to the States Sunday evening, when he could retrieve his wife and escort her to Europe.

Unless Samantha needed him sooner, he'd stick to his original plan. Still, the thought of seeing her held an appeal that rivaled breathing. Their conversations on the phone brightened his day in ways he didn't expect. Their flirting would prove troublesome if they were in the same country. An ocean apart felt safe. Maybe that's why Blake found himself opening up to her. Women had always been a game to be played. First in attracting them, which wasn't hard, and then seducing them. Although he didn't set a time limit with the previous women in his life, he never encouraged relationships to last longer than six months to a year. His attraction usually wavered much sooner than that. Monogamy and Blake were strangers. He'd inherited that one trait from his father.

Samantha didn't need to be played. For the first time in his adult life, honesty with the opposite sex felt safe.

His phone beeped as a text message arrived.

"Sam," he breathed her name. Hoping.

It wasn't her.

He read the message from his bank informing him of activity on the credit card he'd given to his bride.

Maybe Vanessa's visit wasn't a complete waste, he mused. He noticed the amount charged and smiled. Samantha's comment about women being emotional creatures swam in his mind. Apparently, his wife wasn't immune.

Traumatic times in one's life often led to a sixth sense about things. At least that's what Samantha believed. Lord knew she'd shouldered enough drama to last two lifetimes in her short handful of years.

The camera-toting rejects had moved on to the latest imploding starlet whose drug addiction and reckless behavior landed her in jail. Thankfully, they forgot all about the new duchess living in the lowlands of Tarzana. Yet still the heavy weight of being watched, the eyes of someone, followed Samantha around.

And it was starting to piss her off.

The last year of her father's freedom was anything but. Samantha had noticed new students on campus who never seemed to go to class but always managed to cross her path. Dark cars followed her convertible and parked across the street from her hangouts. The phones in her home made a clicking noise whenever she picked up the line. It got to the point where Samantha dressed in her bathroom or the huge walk-in closet to ensure some measure of privacy.

Blake hadn't revealed all the particulars about who would be watching their marriage over the next year, only that someone would. Their time together would need to be convincing, their time apart seem difficult for both of them. She supposed the daily phone calls from Blake were a way of measuring their affection. At least the phone records would reveal a daily conversation.

Samantha convinced Blake that Vanessa's visit hadn't affected her. This was probably the only half-truth Sam had given to her husband to date. No need for him to know how tilted she'd become. Of course, her credit card bill spoke for itself. Julia Roberts's movie character held nothing on Samantha. Designer suits, dresses, shoes, and handbags. She sat in a salon for a half day of manicures, pedicures, facials, and a haircut. A couple of large-brimmed hats and dark sunglasses helped cover her appearance, yet still the creepy sensation of eyes picking her out of a crowd stayed with her.

"You're being paranoid," Samantha told herself as she pulled the shades down early in the afternoon on Friday.

Glancing at her watch, Samantha calculated Blake's time in Europe. He'd done most of the calling, and she thought it would probably look good for her to take the initiative if, in fact, someone was auditing the calls. She picked up the landline and reached for the paper on her desk with his home number.

The dial tone buzzed, clicked, and buzzed again.

Samantha froze in place.

She knew that sound. Remembered it far too well. After dropping the phone back in the cradle, she considered her options. Calling Blake on her cell was one, but for all she knew, a camera watched and a microphone was somewhere in her house. Thank goodness most of her recent conversations with Blake had taken place on her cell outside the house.

Leaving her house and making the call was another option.

Then there was option number three. If the person responsible for bugging her phone was listening and hoping to hear a discussion about a fake marriage, they were going to be very, very disappointed.

The government had invaded her privacy before. The results had been deadly. Although the stakes weren't as high this time, there was no way Samantha was going to allow anyone a chance to take what was rightfully Blake's to keep.

For better or for worse, Blake was her husband—for the next fifty-three weeks, anyway.

Samantha toed off her shoes and removed the cordless phone from the cradle once again. With her cell phone in the other hand, she first sent a text.

Are you home?

Her phone buzzed. *For the first time all week.*

She started dialing his number. *Keep your cell handy and play along.*

Blake stared at the screen of his cell phone and shook his head. "Play along? What's that supposed to mean?" He was about to type in his question when his house phone rang.

When he answered, Samantha's husky bedroom

voice practically purred over the line. "Hi, honey."

Honey? Where had that come from? He opened his mouth to ask, but Samantha kept talking, each syllable more enticing than the next.

"How was your day?"

"Busy. I'm looking forward to half a day off tomorrow." His cell phone buzzed. *Do you hear that click in the line?*

He read Samantha's question and started to answer aloud. "Samantha, what's going—"

"God, I miss you. I wish my passport would hurry up and get here so I can join you."

Blake's eyes shot up. Samantha didn't sound like she'd been drinking, although he did like the thought of her missing him. Still, he knew bullshit when he heard it.

Someone is bugging my phone. Keep talking.

"What?" Bugging her phone?

"I said, I miss you," Samantha's breathless voice wavered.

"I miss you too," he whispered slowly as he typed back. *WTF is going on?*

Samantha chuckled. "You know what I've been thinking about all day?" The 900-number voice collided with the text messages, both of which started to screw with his brain. If someone had bugged her phone, they'd been in her house. His jaw started to ache, and heat built inside his body. He was too damn far away to reach her.

"No, why don't you tell me?"

Being watched. Think someone's listening to us now.

"I've been thinking about that sexy smile of yours."

He hesitated in his text reply. "You think my smile's sexy?"

"You know I do. I miss seeing the laughter in your eyes when we're together."

Blake knew her words were for the person listening, but the effect of them was no less potent. Samantha might not be an actress, but she was doing a hell of a job now.

We need to get you out of there.

"You know what I miss about you?" he asked, keeping the conversation exactly where she'd put it.

"Tell me."

I have to agree with you, she texted.

He was shocked that she'd agreed without a fight. "What?"

"I said, tell me what you miss about me," Samantha redirected him.

Blake set the phone aside and concentrated on her words.

"I miss that wild hair of yours pressed on my pillow." The image was one he pictured often, even if he hadn't seen it—yet. "The way you moisten your lips right before I kiss you."

"You do?" Her voice grew rough.

"I miss the lavender scent of your skin. I'm

80

going to have the gardeners plant bushels of it here so every time I walk by I'll be reminded of you." Where had that come from? And since when was he a poet?

The phone was silent for a moment. "Samantha? Are you still there?" He glanced at his cell to see if she'd sent another text. She hadn't.

"I'm here. I just . . . I need to be closer to you. Maybe I should move into your home in Malibu."

He smiled. "I'm glad you finally agree."

"Everything happened so fast. I thought it would be best to move slowly. Now it just seems silly."

"You're an independent woman. I understand. But we'll be spending time here in Europe and there. It would be better for you to get comfortable in both places. Then at least I'll know where you are when we have to be apart." Funny, every word he said was true, but if there weren't another set of ears listening, he probably wouldn't be saying any of it.

"You're—dammit!" Her expletive exploded from her lips.

The hair on his neck stood on end. "What's wrong?"

"I . . . I stubbed my toe." She sounded pissed, not hurt.

His phone buzzed. *Found a camera.*

"What are you doing?" he asked. He took to his feet and started to pace.

"Picking out a few books to take to your house.

When will you be here on Sunday?" If he hadn't been listening, he wouldn't have noticed the tremor in her voice. He pressed the number to Neil and sent an urgent text: *Get to Sam's now! I'll call you in a few minutes.*

"I'm going to rearrange my plans and fly in sooner." *As in tonight.*

"That isn't necessary," she said.

"I disagree. We've been apart too long." Those words felt exactly right, despite their agreed-upon contract.

She let out a deep breath. "You won't get an argument out of me."

"I'll call later."

"Don't do anything rash," she told him. "I'm fine."

But he wasn't. Someone was spying on his wife, listening to her conversations . . . watching her. And that took trying to catch them in a lie too far.

"I'll be there by morning."

"I'll look forward to it."

Blake smiled and hung up the phone.

Pack what you need for today and tomorrow. Neil is on his way.

He placed a call to his bodyguard, explaining the situation. The next call was to his pilot. He rubbed his frustrated hands through his hair and scrambled to make arrangements to leave. His long-distance marriage no longer felt safe. His brain buzzed with an urgency that kept his toe tapping and his hands wringing to weave around someone's neck. Would his cousin stoop to this level? Or was Vanessa utterly scorned and wanting some crazy revenge? Even Parker and Parker couldn't be eliminated from the short list of suspects, since they stood to gain an extra measure of cash should Blake and Samantha's marriage be exposed as a fraud.

Twenty minutes later, his phone rang en route to the airport.

"Samantha?"

"Yeah, it's me." She sounded worn out. Depleted. "I'm at your place."

"Then it's safe to talk. My security would detect a bug. How are you holding up?"

She sighed. The sound grew heavy in his ear. "I'm pissed. I thought my days of bugged phones and hidden cameras were behind me. Who would go to these lengths, Blake?"

"I've been asking myself that question since you called. I have people working on it. We'll find out."

"Let me know what I can do to help. Whoever is responsible has an enemy in me." The spark in her voice was better than the deflated one of a moment ago. His feisty redheaded wife could be a fireball when cornered.

"I'll be in late tonight. What room did you choose?"

"Oh, ah, I . . . I wasn't sure who knew what around here so I told Neil to put my things in your suite," she stammered. "I can move."

He warmed to the thought of her head on his pillow, her eyes drifting to sleep in his bed. "Don't move. You're right. I trust my staff, but I don't think we should alert them."

"Are you sure?" She sounded vulnerable again. The strong desire to pull her into his arms and envelop her with his strength was painful.

"Please. I insist." He knew better than to demand. Samantha took his commands and tossed them in his face whenever possible. Asking nicely was new to him, but he grew better at the task every day.

"All right. I'll see you in the morning."

His finger tapped along his phone after he hung up. The image of Samantha curled up in a tight little ball on his bed, her eyes wide with fear, choked him. His fingers clutched hard against his palms. Whoever did this had made a huge, costly mistake. He would crush the person who violated his wife's privacy on this level. Paparazzi on public streets, eavesdropping while standing in line at a store—fine. But this? What if there was a camera in her bedroom? What if someone watched her dress, watched her bathe?

No wonder she sounded scared.

The more he thought about it, the harder it was to see anything but red.

. . .

Half-memory, half-dream, Samantha's sleep-filled brain filtered images of her walking through campus, a backpack slung over her shoulder.

Someone followed behind her. She'd seen him before, but couldn't place his face. The panic in her blood started after she'd revealed her deepest thoughts to her business professor.

In the back of Samantha's mind, she knew she was dreaming. Knew where the dream was headed and tried desperately to stop it.

A picture of her childhood bedroom flashed in her mind. A candid conversation with a trusted friend. Her mother, alive, telling her to mind her mouth.

Jordan, just into her training bra, laughing at something their dog, Buster, was doing.

All these images mixed and coiled tight in Samantha's chest.

Two men wearing dark suits and holding a badge removed her from her classroom and questioned her. Only, instead of asking about where her father was, what he was doing, they asked about Blake.

"What he's doing is illegal, Samantha. Thousands of people suffer because of him."

No! She fought the dream, willing the images to change.

They pressed forward, and fear gripped her heart.

Samantha shot up in bed, her breathing rapid and

her heart rate soaring. In a flash, Blake pushed out of the chair he'd been sleeping in and rushed to her side.

"Sam, are you OK?" His hands captured her arms to steady her.

Forcing her breath to slow, she nodded. "Bad dream."

"You're shaking." The words left his mouth, his arms circled around her, and he pulled her to his chest.

She probably should have pushed away but couldn't find the energy. She sucked in the deep pine scent of masculinity that always followed Blake around. This close, it was more potent, powerful. Samantha leaned into him and closed her eyes.

He ran his hands over her back and smoothed her hair. "It's OK," he whispered.

The force of her dream left an imprint on her heart. The memories of her mother alive, her sister whole. All gone.

It was her fault.

Blake held her for what felt like forever. When she lifted her head from his chest, she noticed for the first time he still wore a dress shirt and slacks. His jaw held a day's worth of stubble, and his eyes were heavy with concern. Always sinfully handsome, he still looked tired.

"I'm OK now," she told him.

Even though he moved back, he didn't let go.

His hands traced the outer edges of her arms before grasping her fingers to his.

A strong sense of being anchored, of belonging, washed over her. Blake's eyes rounded over her face, as if searching for physical signs of abuse. His worry for her caught in her throat, and the attraction she'd felt for him swelled inside. As vulnerable as she felt, she knew better than to flirt with him or bring to his attention the fact that she was in his bed, wearing only a light nightgown.

Breaking eye contact, Samantha glanced across the room. "You were sleeping in the chair?"

"I only meant to check on you. I must have drifted off."

But his shoes had been kicked off by the chair, and his coat was folded over the back of it.

"What are we going to do? Someone is taking desperate measures to catch us in this lie."

"They took it too far." His hand tightened on hers.

She squeezed back. "So what do we do now? Leaving the house will only push whoever is behind this away for so long. The Feds' surveillance of our house lasted for over a year while they built their case. We've no way of knowing if someone is watching or listening all the time." The thought of dodging cameras and bugs on phones for a year gave her a headache.

"I'll find out who did this. It's still illegal to penetrate someone's home and record them."

"It might be illegal, but it won't stop them. We need to convince them they're wasting their time. Otherwise, somewhere, somehow, one of us is going to mess up and reveal just how temporary this marriage is. Then you'll lose everything you stand to gain, and it will somehow be my fault."

His eyes narrowed, and he tilted his head in question. "Why your fault? We both said 'I do' for the wrong reasons."

Afraid he'd see her past sins in her eyes, Samantha removed her hands from his and pulled her knees into her chest. Staring at the opposite side of the room, she said, "Maybe it won't be all my fault . . ."

Blake shifted into her line of sight and placed a hand on her knee. The heat of his palm radiated up her leg and snapped her attention to the man sitting beside her. "Now that we know how dirty we're being played, we need to win on their terms. We'll use their cameras to show them how wrong they are about us."

"How do you suggest we do that?"

A tilt of his lips hid a grin. The worry in his eyes started to fade. "You and I'll go to your house and pack your things. Before we get there, I'll send over a team to find any other cameras that might be hiding."

"Won't that be obvious?"

"Was it obvious when whoever planted them did it?"

She'd wondered about that all night. The phone repair guys were the only ones who'd been in her house since she and Blake had gotten married. "No."

"We'll find the cameras and play to them."

Her pulse picked up speed. "Play to them?"

Blake reached out and tucked a strand of her hair behind her ear. The feel of his fingers on her skin sizzled. He felt the current too. She could see it in his beautiful gray eyes. "Would it be so hard to kiss me again? For the camera?"

She licked her lips and watched his as he spoke. "A kiss?"

His palm cupped her cheek. "Maybe some heavy petting. There has to be a room void of cameras where we can escape. Let the person watching wonder."

Oh, she wondered. Wondered what it would feel like in his arms. She'd thought of kissing him again ever since their wedding day.

"What would that prove?" she asked, ignoring how his thumb stroked her cheek and brought erotic images of his hands on other parts of her body.

"It would prove we're intimate, that we enjoy each other outside of the public eye. As long as they think we're oblivious of their surveillance, it should work. What do you say, Samantha? Are you up for the challenge?"

She stopped staring at his lips and found him

staring at her. He already knew how to get her riled and ready for a fight. "I'm up for it."

His grin turned into a huge smile. "Atta girl. Now, why don't you have the cook make you breakfast while I try to catch a couple hours sleep? Then we'll take a trip to your place. That should give my men the time they need to find all the bugs."

He dropped his hand to his side and pushed off the bed.

"Blake? What about tomorrow? The next day? How are we going to keep this up for a year?"

"One day at a time, sweetheart. We're two intelligent people with the same goal. We'll figure something out."

Chapter Six

There were cameras in her living room, kitchen, and both bedrooms. They knew about the phone line already. According to Blake's men, her car was clean.

But dammit! Someone had watched her dress, watched her sleep. Samantha revealed to Blake the conversation she'd had with Eliza, the only one that might hold a hint of their deceptive marriage. The cameras were most likely planted by the guys posing as telephone repairmen. Or perhaps someone had snuck in while she'd been out jogging.

After that, the conversations had all been on her cell phone and usually when she'd been out. Not that it mattered. They'd only talked about the reception and the people she'd meet. Admittedly, they talked like an old married couple, which was surprising considering they hardly knew each other.

Blake drove the town car with Sam guiding the way to her house.

As the townhome drew closer, the reality of what they were doing spread worry throughout her limbs.

"You're wringing your hands together," Blake told her. "What's wrong?"

"Honest answer?" she asked him, knowing what he'd say.

"Always."

"Kissing you."

He snuck a glance behind his glasses and returned his eyes to the road. "Kissing me is wrong?"

"Yes," she blurted out. "I mean, no."

He chuckled. "Which is it?"

"Ugh. What if I choke? What if I don't look convincing?" What if she screwed up and gave the camera exactly what they wanted and Blake lost his inheritance?

Blake removed one hand from the steering wheel and placed it over her cold ones. "Samantha?"

"Yes."

"Relax. Let me take charge here."

She shook her head. "I'm not used to men taking charge in my life."

"I know that. But you can trust me."

She wanted to trust him. But her hands shook as they pulled into her driveway. He removed the key from the ignition and shifted in his seat. "Let's just go inside and start packing."

"Are you going to kiss me the minute we're inside?" God, she had to know so she could prepare herself.

Blake leaned forward and removed his sunglasses. "Come here," he whispered, staring at her lips.

She inched forward, thinking he wanted to whisper something important.

Instead, he leaned over the seat and placed his lips softly on hers. The heat was instant and sizzled all the way to her toes. Her eyes fluttered shut as she eased into his kiss. Then he moved away. "Kissing will be the easy part," he said over her opened lips. "Pulling back will prove much harder."

Blake brushed his thumb over her lower lip before turning and opening his door.

Samantha stepped on wobbly legs and allowed Blake to hold her arm for support.

He glanced up and down the block, giving it an obviously disapproving glare. "This neighborhood doesn't feel safe to me. How long have you lived here?"

"Two years," she told him as she placed her key in the lock and opened the door.

They stepped inside the foyer, and Samantha placed her purse on the table. "I have some boxes in a shed out back."

"I'll get the ones from the car."

As they went in opposite directions, Samantha found her eyes traveling to the camera she knew was hidden in her bookcase. Walking by it, she headed out through her kitchen to the shed and came back with several dusty cardboard boxes in various sizes. She dumped them on the coffee table and glanced around the room.

Blake brought in half a dozen boxes, still folded up, and a roll of packing tape.

"Why don't we use those for my clothes since they're clean?" she suggested.

"OK," he said glancing up the stairwell.

Samantha led the way to her bedroom and had Blake dump the boxes on her bed. He picked them up one by one and tucked their edges together. After a little tape, the boxes were ready to go.

"Where do you want me to start?" Blake asked.

"In the closet."

After several minutes of packing, Samantha forgot all about the cameras and found her head deep inside her dresser. She grabbed a simple band and tied her hair back, out of the way.

"Should I be worried about all these shoes in here?" Blake asked from her closet.

She laughed. "You're the one who told me to go shopping," she teased.

"Looks like I'll be hiring a handyman to build another walk-in just for you." There was laughter in his voice.

"Women love clothes."

"And shoes, apparently. God, I didn't think anyone needed this many."

Samantha tucked her panties into a box and reached for more. "I'm short, in case you haven't noticed. I need heels to see how the rest of you live."

Blake's voice moved closer. "You're not short," he said.

She turned to see him holding a pair of four-inch pumps.

"Vertically challenged, then." She stood to prove her point. "See?" Beside him, the top of her head met his chin. "Short!"

His eyes seemed to drag her into his frame. "I wouldn't change anything about you," he told her. Blake reached out and tugged the band from her hair. His fingers brushed over the ends, and Samantha forgot to breathe. The closer he moved into her personal space, the less air was available for her lungs. She tilted her head as he moved in, and allowed his mouth to move over hers. Blake's hand dropped the shoes and wrapped around her waist, holding her close.

Her breasts pushed against the hard plane of his chest as Blake angled his head to deepen their kiss. Only when his tongue licked her lips open did she remember the cameras pointed at them. She stiffened, but Blake didn't let her go. Instead, he glided his hand down her back and rounded over her behind.

Her body buzzed, and his tongue started a slow dance with hers. His pine scent and heated breath easily distracted her from everything but the feeling of him holding her, touching her.

Liquid started to pool in her belly as desire swept up her spine. She hadn't been kissed in so long she'd forgotten how good it felt. And had it ever felt this good? She didn't think so.

Blake moaned, or maybe she did, as his lips left hers and started to trail over her jaw, her neck. He might be playing for the camera, but his body didn't know the rules. The heat of his erection sat against her belly, displaying a need she felt.

"I missed you," he whispered in her hair.

Samantha reached around his shoulders and clawed at the edges of his shirt. "I missed you too."

His eyes caught hers, and the sparkle of mischief there made her smile. When her hand found the bare flesh of his back, his eyes darkened. He kissed her again, this time with more desperation. She felt his hand cup her breast through the fabric of her shirt. She wanted to feel him closer, wanted him to taste her skin where his hands wandered.

"Oh God," she whispered. *This is dangerous.* Their desire was real, or at least it was for her.

"You know what I want?" he asked when he let her lips go.

"What?" She kissed his jaw and started to undo the buttons on his shirt.

Blake bent down and lifted her into his arms.

She squealed and grasped his shoulders to avoid falling.

"I want to have you in the shower."

Samantha smiled and crossed her ankles as Blake walked them out of the room and away from those prying eyes.

When they reached the bathroom door, he placed her back on her feet and took her lips again. The back of her legs bumped into the cheap Formica countertop as they squeezed into the small space. Blake lifted her until she sat next to her sink. All the while, his lips kept dancing with hers. He wedged himself between her thighs, and her hips rocked forward to find more contact.

The sound of the door closing registered in a small corner of her brain, but her lips kept themselves glued to Blake's.

They were alone. No cameras, no watchful eyes.

The soft comfort of Blake's mouth left hers and came to rest on her temple. She whimpered at the loss. He kept his arms wrapped around her body, kept her tucked firmly in his embrace. Reality slowly seeped in as they both searched for control.

She shouldn't have been so at home in his arms. How was she going to stay out of his bed if they continued to play Russian roulette? Samantha started to pull away but Blake held on.

"I need a minute," he breathed into her ear, his voice rough with desire.

She leaned into him and loosened her grip on his broad shoulders. For several minutes, they stood still, neither talking. Blake ran his hands up and down her back with slow, even strokes.

"Shouldn't we turn on the shower?" she finally asked, not sure if Blake was ever going to let her go.

Blake's smoky gaze met hers and his brow lifted. "Is that an invitation?"

"For the camera," she said in a rush.

Was that disappointment flashing in his eyes? "Right." He shook his head and pushed himself away from her arms. The room chilled instantly.

The tiny bathroom didn't leave much room for either of them, so Samantha stayed on the counter and watched as Blake turned on the water in the shower. When he turned toward her and rested his back against the door, he attempted a smile, but it didn't reach his eyes.

"This is crazy, isn't it?" she asked him, wanting desperately to know what his thoughts were.

He ran a hand through his hair in a gesture Sam started to recognize as a sign of stress. "What's crazy is how much I want you, and how much effort we're going through to convince people we're sleeping together when we're not."

She tried smiling, to lighten the mood. "When you put it that way, we sound certifiable."

The steam from the shower started to fill the room. For the first time since they'd met, silence stretched before them as big as the Grand Canyon.

"How long should we stay in here?"

Blake glanced at the shower stall as if it held the answer to her question. "Well, if I were in there making love to you, I'd spend a lot of time learning every inch of your body."

Samantha sucked in her lower lip and pictured his lips licking paths and creating friction. "Talk like that is going to get us both in trouble."

"Why are we sitting out here and letting all that hot water run down the drain, again?"

Hell if she knew. Oh yeah. They were married, and being intimate wasn't in their plans.

"Because we're both mercenaries, and sleeping together isn't part of the overall plan. Impulsive actions could ruin everything." Her words made sense, but her heart wasn't listening. The room filled with steam, and her clothes started to stick to her frame.

"We can change the plan," he suggested.

Her body tingled with the possibility. "Are you suggesting a yearlong affair?" Could she do that?

Now his smile reached higher and lit his eyes. "We're both adults with an obvious attraction."

Which still boggled her mind. What could Blake possibly see in her? Compared to Vanessa or Jackie—*excuse me, Jacqueline*—Samantha was a black duck in a pond filled with white swans. Maybe he was realizing that marriage to her for a year was going to put a serious dent in his sex life.

"I've never embarked on an affair with an end date in mind."

"Neither have I." As he spoke, he moved closer, his hand coming to rest on the counter beside her.

"Right! Then why is it your relationships never last longer than six to nine months?"

"Coincidence."

"Liar."

His eyes widened in fake horror. "You wound me."

"It would take more than that to wound you."

Blake ran a finger over her chin and lower lip. "You know me so well already. We're a lot alike, Samantha. What would be wrong with a satisfying physical relationship that had a beginning and an end?"

His gaze lowered to her lips, and he slid closer. The undeniable pull of the man made it hard to think. And that was the problem. Sex was clouding her brain just like the fog in the room. She may have married him for money, but could she keep her heart out of it if they started sleeping together? "Are you this convincing in all your business deals?"

"Am I convincing you?" His hands found her waist, and his fingers kneaded her flesh.

"Asking me now when I'm keyed up isn't fair. You know that, right?"

His other hand came to rest on her thigh and started a slow ascent. "I seldom play fair. And I never play when I don't think I'll win."

It was a warning, one she really needed to heed.

Reluctantly, Samantha stopped his hand from moving up her leg. "I'll think about it," she told him, because saying no wouldn't have been possible and saying yes was reckless.

Blake let a grateful smile linger on his lips. "I'll take that."

She pushed against his chest, hopped down from the counter, and started to pull her shirt over her head.

"Done thinking already?"

Samantha rolled her eyes and flung her shirt to the floor. Underneath was a pink lacy bra. "Give me your shirt," she demanded.

"What?" Blake's eyes never left her breasts. *Men are so easy.* A set of boobs rendered them speechless.

"Your shirt."

He blinked, twice, three times, and then unbuttoned his white dress shirt to reveal a span of pure masculine chest.

Tearing her eyes away, Samantha moved around Blake and pushed the shower curtain back. The water had turned cold while they spoke, which served her well. Keeping the rest of her body out of the water, she ducked her head under the spray and shivered as the water wet her hair.

"What are you doing?"

Poor Blake was having a hard time catching up. The fact she'd managed to keep him in a semi–state of confusion brought a wave of feminine pleasure over her. "Sorry you missed it, but we just made love in the shower. Leaving here dry would be a dead giveaway." Her eyes drifted down his frame to his obvious state of arousal pressing inside his slacks. "That and . . . other things."

Blake glanced down and moaned.

Samantha pushed her arms into his shirt. After buttoning it up, she carefully removed her bra and then leaned down to remove her jeans. When she kicked free of her clothes and straightened to her full height, Blake's eyes were riddled with desire so thick she felt sorry for him. The cool water dripping off her hair and down her back did a decent job of chilling her libido.

"You're wicked." Blake's hungry words made her laugh.

He reached for her, but she squealed and managed to duck away. He let his hands drop.

"Take a cold shower, Blake. I said I'd think about it."

"I'll get naked and we can think about it together."

She laughed. "Even if I decided to go for your completely foolish proposal, I wouldn't act on it now, not with a camera in the next room."

Blake scrubbed his hands down both sides of his face. "But we're trying to convince whoever is watching that we did. Why not just—"

"Not gonna happen," she cut him off. "Take a cold shower." Wearing her underwear and Blake's shirt, Samantha slipped from the bathroom and smiled as she continued with her packing.

They packed a minimum of things, mainly clothes and personal items Samantha needed immediately.

Then Blake suggested they hire a moving company to do the rest. He went out of his way to mention his intention in front of the camera in her living room. With any luck, whoever planted the surveillance cameras would scramble to remove them before the movers had a chance of finding them.

Neil had already hired some friends to watch the house and follow and record whoever came and went. They might get lucky, find the culprits, and put an end to their watchful eyes.

Back at his Malibu home, Blake informed his staff that any and everything Samantha needed was to be taken care of immediately. She had complete charge of his house and he expected her to be treated like the duchess she was. He considered her small role here a launching pad for what was to come.

"It's been a long time since I had a maid," Sam told him once they were alone.

"I can't have my wife doing housework." He was prepared for her fight and smiled when she didn't challenge him.

"I never liked mopping floors. You'll get no argument from me."

Such blatant honesty about the simplest of things pleased him.

"You won't have time for that anyway," he informed her. They sat out on the veranda and watched the sun setting over the Pacific.

"Why's that?"

"I need you to talk to the caterers and designers about the reception at Albany Hall."

"You want me to plan a party for a place I've never been, for people I've never met?"

Blake sent her a sympathetic look. "I need you to approve what they come up with. I trust my staff there completely, but I need them to be prepared to ask you about these things when we get there. It's best we start that relationship now."

She stretched her legs out on the chaise and tucked them under a blanket. "Is this the first party you've thrown at your home?"

"No."

"Then who planned them before? I can't see you doing it."

Her mind was so sharp. "My mother did most of the party planning." Although his mother would want to continue planning everything in his ancestral home, he wanted to make certain Samantha had a choice about everything.

Sam's curiosity didn't sit long before she started asking more questions. "Where does your mother live?"

"Albany Hall."

"She lives in your house?" There was a small amount of surprise in Sam's voice.

Blake wondered how much he should reveal, how much truth he could trust to his wife. He started with the facts that Samantha could easily obtain if she bothered looking.

"My mother was the Duchess of Albany all the time she'd been married to my father. After his death, she kept the title until I married you."

"Ouch. Talk about a wedge between a mother and a daughter-in-law. This can't be a good thing."

Blake shifted in his seat to look at his wife. "It's expected. She knew the day would come sooner than later. Once my father's will was read, I'm sure she realized I'd do everything in my power to secure my inheritance."

"How close are you and your mother?"

"We do OK."

"That doesn't sound hopeful."

The air around him started to chill. There was a time when he and his mother had been close. When their common goal had been hating his father. "You don't have to worry about her."

Samantha seemed to gather the information, process it, and then kick out a solid assessment. "But there is someone I need to worry about, isn't there?"

He wanted to lie, but couldn't. With Sam, it felt wrong to let white lies begin and possibly wedge between them. "My cousin. He's on my short list of people who might have planted those cameras in your home."

"You're kidding."

"I wish I were. Howard stands to inherit a hefty sum should our marriage fail."

"I take it the two of you aren't chummy."

"Barely tolerate each other is a better description. He stays at Albany as often as he can manage. My mother is too kind to send him away."

"Why don't you?"

"I'm not there enough to care. Though, now that will change."

"How so?" Samantha said.

"My mother has the right to live in the house until the estate turns over to me next year. It's understood that once I take a wife, she assumes the duties of duchess, and my mother will move to the smaller estate on the grounds." He didn't expect Sam to take all this in and understand it, but he wanted her to grasp most of it before they left for Europe.

"I don't think I've done enough research on your family home. I assumed Albany Hall was a convenient name for a manor house. Something you British use to make things grander than they are." Samantha played with a lock of her hair as she spoke. Her eyes kept drifting toward the sea.

"Once you see Albany Hall, you'll understand my reluctance to choose a bride."

"Hmm, you know, something has bothered me since we met."

"What's that?"

"Why don't you have a British accent? You grew up there, right?"

Memories of hearing his father scold him for not speaking properly chased around in his head. Blake did everything he could to go against his father's wishes, right down to speaking American English and not the Queen's English.

"I spent summers at Albany when I was in boarding school. Every chance we could, my mother brought my sister and me here to the States. I immersed myself in American culture." Blake noticed the fog bank drifting closer as his mind drifted with it. "I rebelled against my father on many levels."

"Do you think that dissension between the two of you prompted him to make it more difficult to collect your inheritance?"

Blake gave a curt shake of his head. "My father had to have the last word. Even in death."

"Was he that awful in life?"

"My father was a typical British royal. Old money filled his pockets and awarded him with the ability to be a pompous jackass whenever he wanted. He married my mother knowing he'd be unfaithful." He remembered the first time he'd seen his mother crying over his father's infidelity. A British tabloid had splashed his father's face over the cover, with a woman ten years younger on his arm. That was when the trips to America began to shape Blake's life. "He thought he was entitled to walk on people."

"Why didn't your mother leave him?" The softness in Samantha's voice forced Blake's attention away from the sea. Her bright-green eyes watched him through lowered lashes, as if she were an intruder carefully trying to avoid detection.

"I don't know. Money, probably. They never spoke of divorce. They lived separate lives most of the time. After my sister was born, they stopped sleeping in the same room."

"So was your hatred for how your father treated your mother what pushed the two of you apart?"

Did he really hate his father? Blake had never put such a strong word to his emotions. He didn't like the man, no doubt about that. "My father wanted me to be just like him. 'Go to school, get an education, but don't think you have to work more than a day a week.'" Blake let his father's accent bleed into his mockery.

A sad smile spread over Samantha's face. "So your rebellion was to make your own fortune."

Blake sat taller. "I funneled my allowance into stock in the shipping company I now own. Halfway through college, I made my first million. My father was furious."

"He wanted to control you," Samantha said. "He couldn't do that if you were a self-made man."

Blake stared at his wife and had an over-whelming sense of pride. He couldn't remember anyone ever diving this deeply into his past and concluding everything so perfectly. Samantha listened and truly heard what he said. "Exactly."

"Tell me, then, why work so hard to hold on to his money? It isn't like you need it."

"I considered walking away. But my sister, who only knows the lifestyle we were raised in, and also my mother, for that matter, they don't deserve to have their lives ripped away. Not to mention we're talking a hell of a lot of money." He laughed, trying to put the somber walk down memory lane behind them.

Samantha appeared to simmer over the information for a few minutes as the last rays of the sun sizzled into the ocean. "You know something, Blake?" she asked, as her eyes left his and stared into the fading sun.

"What?"

"I'm starting to think you're more martyr than mercenary."

He huffed out a laugh, reached over, and took her hand in his. "This coming from a woman who married me to secure her sister's care."

Samantha snapped out of her haze and squeezed his hand. "Oh no. Jordan." She started to push up from her comfortable position.

"What is it?"

"It's Saturday. I forgot about my weekly visit with my sister." Samantha pulled her hand out of his. "I've got to go."

"Isn't it too late?"

Samantha waved his question away. "Of course not." She sent him a curious glance. "Do you want to come with me? See where all your money's going?"

Blake had a dozen things he should have been doing instead of revealing his past to his wife. He didn't want to do any of it. "I'd love to meet your sister."

Chapter Seven

"This place is amazing." Eliza spun full circle in the middle of Blake's formal living room. "I can't believe you didn't jump at living here the minute you guys came back from Vegas."

"It didn't feel right."

"But it does now? What's changed?" Eliza flopped down on an overstuffed sofa and crossed her legs.

Samantha lowered her voice even though the cook was busy preparing their lunch and the maid was upstairs doing God knew what. Blake needed to spend the day in his office, which left Sam with little to do. "We're getting more comfortable together, I guess. The security here isn't something I could manage in Tarzana."

"You got that right. That Neil guy is kinda scary if you ask me." Eliza had walked around the bulky man when he met her at her car.

"He doesn't say much."

"He didn't say anything to me. Just stared at me."

"Blake insists he's harmless to those who aren't messing with him." Samantha found herself in one of the Queen Anne chairs facing her friend. The soft silk pantsuit she wore drifted over her skin and made her feel like she wasn't wearing anything at all. With the extra time on her hands, Sam took more time getting dressed in the morning, more time preening for her day.

When Blake had joined her at Moonlight, Samantha faced the full force of being in a marriage to a man as rich and handsome as her husband. He charmed the staff and won more than a few smiles from her sister. Ever since Jordan's stroke, her ability to express her needs had been difficult. Expressive aphasia was what the doctors called her condition. To keep her sister from being overly anxious and frustrated, Sam often finished Jordan's sentences for her. Blake seemed to understand the situation and worked hard to ask yes or no questions and avoided subjects that would bring on stress.

On their way out, Blake found an administrator, and like a switch, his charm turned off and the business side of him shone through. He wanted to know about security in the home, how they kept Jordan safe from strangers walking into her room, and who was by her side when it wasn't meal-time. A rapid stream of questions, which he could have asked Samantha, were fired off and answered before she could interrupt. His sincerity over her sister's care and safety kept Sam from being upset with him. Yet, after they'd left, when he started to question the home's ability to care for Jordan properly, Samantha became defensive.

"It's the best home for people in Jordan's situation. Most homes are geared for older Alzheimer patients. Moonlight specializes in younger patients with developmental problems."

"Why not care for her at home?"

Of course, that would have been ideal, but Samantha couldn't afford that kind of round-the-clock in-home care. "I couldn't."

She'd tried to do it on her own before but failed. Once Blake realized how upset the conversation was making her, he'd had the good sense to drop the subject.

"I'm glad Neil is on your side. I wouldn't want to be that man's enemy," Eliza said, snapping Samantha out of her thoughts. "So, what are we going to do with Alliance?"

She'd given a lot of thought as to how to proceed with her business. The fact was that taking on the role of being Blake Harrison's wife would take up the majority of her time and leave her jet-setting all over the globe. As it was, her passport had arrived first thing that Monday morning, and she and Blake were arranging their departure for early Wednesday.

"I have a proposition for you." She waited until Eliza turned her eyes to her before starting. "I've worked too hard to lose everything I've worked for with Alliance, but I'm obviously going to be unavailable over the next few months."

"I thought you guys were going to live on different continents."

Sam shook her head. "Our original plan isn't going to work the way we'd hoped. In light of the bugs and surveillance cameras, we think it's best to stay close to each other." Samantha's mind shifted to Blake's proposal. He hadn't pushed her to sleep with him since their time in her bathroom, but he'd sent her several heated glances and sexy comments to let her know he still wanted her in his bed. As it was, Samantha slept in the room beside her husband's and told the staff she wasn't feeling well. The excuse was lame, but no one commented.

"Where does that leave Alliance?"

"What would you say to coming in as my partner?"

Eliza's eyes widened and a smile formed on her lips. "What would that look like?"

"I'd need you to do some of the fieldwork." They both knew that meant Eliza would need to attend gatherings where women searched for rich husbands, high-profile events where those with money played. Socializing was the best way of gathering prospective clients. Word of mouth worked better than any ad in the paper. "Karen already agreed to introduce you to some of her old friends to get you set up."

"Karen is the one who runs Moonlight, right?"

The knockout, gorgeous blonde whom Blake hadn't looked at twice. Sam nodded. "When you have a new contact, fax the information to me and I'll start the background check on them. I can initiate that from anywhere in the world. What I can't do is meet with people until my time becomes my own again."

"When do you expect that?"

"A few months. Maybe sooner."

Eliza seemed to juggle the new prospect in her mind. "I guess it would be bad form to be talking about temporary marriages after your Vegas wedding to Blake. People might ask questions."

"It wouldn't look good. I'll place things in your name so it looks like I'm your employee." Because any lawyer worth a damn would figure it out otherwise.

"You'd do that?"

"I trust you. And when I offered a partnership, I meant it. If things become too difficult for you when I'm away, we'll hire a temporary secretary. If things pick up, we'll hire a full-time one. We'll split the profits down the middle, and while I'm playing duchess, I'll pay for the expenses."

Eliza's eyes lit up. "As in fancy dresses and dinners with clients?"

Samantha laughed. "I'm sure we can come up with a reasonable budget."

"I'm not sure what to say?"

"Say yes."

"But this is your baby. You've worked hard and I'm new on the scene."

Uncrossing her legs, Sam sat forward and placed

a hand over her friend's. "You helped me when times were hard and never bitched when money was tight."

"You offered me a room at your house. Kinda hard to bitch when you let me live with you for nothing."

Sam waved her off. "I may have started this business, but it has taken both of us to get it where it is today. I don't trust anyone else but you, Eliza."

The slow movement of Eliza's head ended in a full nod and a smile. "How can a girl say no to that?"

"Good."

"Mrs. Harrison?" the cook called from the entryway to the living room.

"Yes, Mary?"

"Your lunch is ready. Would you like it in here, or should I leave it in the dining room?"

Eliza's sly smile told Samantha how impressed she was. "We'll take it in there. I hope you'll join us."

Mary's eyes widened in alarm. "Oh, no, I couldn't do that."

Samantha and Eliza both stood and walked toward Mary. "Oh, yes, you can." Sam laughed as she spoke. "I don't expect you to cook lunch, then eat alone."

"But—"

"Besides, Blake's birthday is in less than a week, and to tell you the truth, I've absolutely no idea what to buy him. Maybe you can help."

Mary's mouth rounded to a perfect *O*. She stopped arguing and followed Sam and her new business partner into the dining room.

Halfway through their meal, Samantha realized how quickly she'd fallen back into the role of a woman with money. She stalled as she ate, remembering how quickly it could all collapse. In her situation, it would. Her and Blake's arrangement was temporary, with a definite beginning and a specific end. She'd have to lock those thoughts away for another year or risk exposing her short-term marriage to anyone who looked.

And in order to lock it away, she needed to start acting like a married woman, she mused.

A happily married woman.

Blake drove through the gates of his Malibu estate two hours past the time he'd told Samantha he'd be home. With the upset in the Middle East, a few of his shipping routes needed to be diverted to avoid the international turmoil. It would have been easier handling the company's current crisis if he'd been in Europe, but Blake had grown used to shuffling things between both continents. Now, with Samantha in his life, he had an even better reason to filter more of his work to the States.

When he'd called her at five thirty to tell her he'd be late, she'd sounded disappointed. That disappointment prompted him to move faster so he could manage a little time with her before she retired for the evening. He had a genuine desire to get to know Samantha better.

There weren't any games with his wife. Her blatant honesty, right down to the statement "I want to sleep with you," was refreshing.

The memory of her shedding her shirt and kicking off her jeans left him hard every time he thought about it. The urge to have his wife in his bed and begging for his touch was irresistible. Although he'd promised to give her time to think about his offer, that didn't mean he wouldn't try seduction to get what he wanted. Hell, she wanted him too. He'd seen it in her sideways glances when she didn't think he was watching and in the way she licked her lips while she stared at his.

Blake had purposely avoided kissing her since she'd moved in. Yet every touch, every time he helped her out of a car or placed his hand on the small of her back to guide her through a door, was torture.

He couldn't wait to explore their volatile attraction and see just how high it would explode.

Walking inside his home, Blake had a strong urge to yell, *Hi, honey, I'm home*. He smiled at the thought and walked through the quiet halls until the soft glow of candlelight in the dining room caught his attention.

Samantha sat at the table wearing a delicate silk

ruby dress and a smile. Her hair cascaded over her shoulders like a soft curtain. Her eyes sparkled as she watched him walk into the room.

Then the smell of succulent beef met his nose and reminded him he hadn't eaten since noon.

Samantha lifted a glass of red wine and rose from her seat before walking toward him.

"What's all this?" he asked as his gaze followed the slim lines of her figure. Her breasts pushed up against the neckline of her dress, exposing her creamy flesh. Her legs, the ones she always complained were too short, peeked through the slit of her dress and towered above four-inch heels that did amazing things to her calves. He decided he liked women's shoes. A second closet was a small price to pay for the sexy view.

"I thought it would be nice to dine alone while we could. Your home in Europe sounds very . . . full."

Blake took the glass she offered and listened for the sounds of Mary in the kitchen or Louisa in the hall. He didn't hear anything other than the faint sound of the ocean through an open window. "We're alone?"

"I gave Mary and Louisa the night off."

He liked the sound of that. The sultry look under Samantha's hooded gaze brought several questions to the tip of his tongue. He tabled them and followed her lead. If she'd decided to take him up on his affair offer, he'd find out soon enough.

"I'm sure they didn't argue."

Samantha pulled out his chair and encouraged him to sit.

"All they asked is what time they should be here in the morning."

"In the morning? They live here."

Samantha removed the lid from one of the serving plates and steam escaped. She piled the plate in front of him with roast and trimmed it with scalloped potatoes and asparagus tips. "Louisa has a boyfriend who was more than happy to put her up for the night."

"I didn't know she had a boyfriend."

"And Mary was happy to visit her grandson and daughter."

Samantha finished serving them both and sat beside him before picking up her fork. His concentration on his food was nonexistent with the lavender smell of her skin so close. "And Neil?"

"He's in his cottage. I asked him to give us some privacy."

Blake felt his stomach rumble and his body heat up. "Why do we need privacy, Samantha?" He slid a sly glance out of the corner of his eye and picked up his fork.

"I thought it would be a nice change." She speared her vegetables with her fork and brought them to the tip of her tongue for a taste. As the asparagus disappeared into the cavern of her mouth, and her eyes caught his, all concerns of where their night would end escaped.

The question was, would they eat before . . . or after?

Blake moaned as she delicately bit the tip of her food and worked her jaw in a slow chewing pattern.

Moisture fled his mouth. Blake kept his eyes glued to his wife as he reached for his wine.

Forcing his fork to pick up food and his mouth to open, he took two bites to her one.

"How was your day?" Her innocent question was asked after she'd licked the rim of her wine-glass before taking a drink.

"Fine." Was that his voice?

She smiled, knowing damn well the effect she had on him. Then she took a sip of her wine and a bite of her food. Her lips moved slowly, reducing Blake's brain to rubble. Eating a meal had never been more seductive.

He ate quickly.

Unable to put one more bite in his mouth, Blake tipped the rest of his wine down his throat and set the glass down hard.

Samantha's innocent smile and mock surprise added to the sexual tension surrounding them both. "Is everything OK?"

He stood, his chair sliding back without cere-mony. "Oh, everything is perfectly fine."

She reached for her wine, but he caught her hand

midway and pulled her to her feet. He didn't offer her any escape before crushing his lips to hers. Like him, she greedily accepted his tongue in her mouth and offered up hers as well.

She tasted like wine and smelled like spring. Blake angled his mouth and deepened their kiss. The grip of her hands clutching his shirt soon relaxed, opened, and she spread them over his chest before encircling his back. Samantha whimpered and melted into his arms. Every touch from this woman was real and alive with desire. She matched him perfectly. Her fight for control, even now, was exciting and new. No one ever drove his relationships. Blake never gave them the reins. With Samantha, he could loosen his hold and trust that she'd drive them both into safe waters.

As Samantha pushed his jacket off his shoulders, he removed his lips from hers so he could breathe, allowing himself a glance into the passionate green eyes of the woman in his arms. "You're beautiful."

Unlike any other time he'd offered her a compliment, he thought this time she believed him.

Nimble fingers started to tug at his tie as Blake backed her to the far end of the dining room table, away from their plates and food. His tie fell to the floor, and Samantha leaned forward, licking and nibbling her way over his chin and neck. Her sexy bedroom voice spoke between bites. "I've thought about your latest proposal."

More than thought about it.

Running his hand over her shoulder, he loosened the sleeve of her dress and pressed his lips to the flesh between her shoulder and neck. So sweet. "Come to any conclusions?" he asked, playing her game, but knowing the score.

His teeth caught the lobe of her ear, and her body shuddered. In his mind, he filed away the information about the spot on her body, noting it sent a bolt of pleasure through her. He vowed to find more places before the night was finished.

"I . . . I decided I'm a mercenary and not a masochist."

He licked the back of her ear.

"Oh God, do that again."

He smiled over her neck and did as she asked. The feel of her leg rubbing against his and her hips searching for friction caused every muscle in his body to strain for her touch. Had he ever been so in need of a woman before? Even in his sex-coated brain, he wanted to be absolutely sure Samantha wanted the same things he did.

Blake buried his hands in her hair and forced her gaze to his. "Are you sure about this, Samantha?"

Her eyes searched his. "Yes," she whispered.

His heart kicked in his chest. "I'm asking for more than one night."

Leaning back, she lifted a hand to his cheek.

"Good. One night won't be enough. I want the full year."

With his gaze zeroed in on the green depths of her eyes, Blake sealed their newest crazy deal with a slow, sizzling kiss.

Blake lifted her hips and set her on the table before moving between her thighs. He found the bare flesh at her knee and traveled up the silky span of her leg. Everywhere he touched, he wanted to taste, to feel her response. She tugged his lower lip into her mouth, and his mind envisioned her using her mouth on much more pleasurable parts of his anatomy.

Samantha clawed at his shirt until she had every button undone, and her hands fanned over him. Her fingers flicked his nipples before she released his mouth and bent down to taste him there. His mind grew dizzy as she played with his body. Her legs wound around his waist, and the heat of her core pressed against his erection. With one long breath, Blake drew her scent deep inside him.

As he started to slide the zipper of her dress down, he opened his eyes and noticed the hard surface of the table where she sat. It wouldn't do for their first time together to happen among the dirty dishes.

While Samantha licked and kissed his flesh, he easily lifted her off the table.

She giggled and wrapped her legs more tightly

around him, then clasped her hands around his shoulders. Walking to the nearest couch was more erotic than he thought possible. Every step brought the heat of her body sliding against him, a jolt of pleasure urging him on.

Damn house was too big. It took entirely too much time to press her into a soft couch and cover her body with his. His shirt went in one direction, her dress in another. Blake stared on at the swell of her ample breasts pushed against a black lacy bra. "So beautiful." He played with her breast through the fabric, making her nipple pebble beneath his touch. He hesitated before revealing her tender flesh and dipped in for his first taste.

Samantha arched into him, pushing her breast deeper inside his mouth. "Please, Blake." Her hips tilted higher, reaching for him.

He wanted to learn her body, find every sensitive spot, and worship it. But Samantha was tugging at his pants, finding the zipper, and reaching inside. When she wrapped her hand around his throbbing erection, she stole his breath. He forgot about her breast, about the fact she still wore panties, and thought of nothing more than plunging deep inside her folds.

The soft texture of her hand held him firmly. Her lips kissed his neck. "I need you," she whispered with her deep, sexy voice.

"You'll have me," he promised as he forced his body away from hers long enough to kick his pants free, his shoes and boxers. While he scrambled to disrobe, Samantha wiggled her slim hips and twisted off her lace panties.

Blake dug a condom out of his wallet and quickly covered himself. When he turned back to her, Samantha had bent one knee, resting her leg against the back of the couch. She reached out to pull him back into her embrace.

He wedged himself between the comfort of her thighs and found her lips for another kiss. She drove her tongue deeper, not letting him gain a breath. Blake knew she'd be passionate, had fantasized about her in bed since they'd met, but this was more than he could have ever wanted.

The tip of his need pushed close to her wet core, hungry for her. When Samantha wrapped her leg around his waist, giving him all the position he needed to please them both, he slid home.

The mewling noise she made when he was buried deep inside her tight body pumped his ego.

"So good," she said after tearing her lips away. Hot, fast breaths escaped her lungs, and her hips started to move.

Better than good. Being in her arms was perfect. Blake's desire to make Samantha writhe with pleasure, pleasure he would bring her, forced him to hold back all thoughts of his own release.

"You're tight," he told her.

His gaze caught hers. Her lips parted with

passion, her heartbeat pulsing at her neck. "Advantage to being small."

But it was more than that. After, once they were both sated, he'd ask about her past, about the men in her life. Right now, it was all about touchin her, pleasing her.

When her fingers dug into his shoulders, then rounded over his ass, her breath kicked higher, and he knew he'd found the rhythm she needed.

"Yes," she moaned. "Right there."

Hips rocking, he forced his release back, waiting for the moment Samantha plunged over the cliff. When she did, she called out his name and strained closer, her body pulsating around him in a tight cocoon. Blake released the tight hold on his control and followed her into heaven.

The weight of Blake's body pressed her into the sofa, and his breathing sounded as ragged as hers. She stretched her leg and ran it down the backside of his. She couldn't stop smiling. Even when the tremors of pleasure simmered to a twitch, she held him close.

Yeah, like she could have said no to this. And to think, she'd have access to his amazing body and sexual talents for an entire year. The eventual end to their relationship made her pause, but she pushed the images of saying good-bye away and focused on the scent and feel of the man still buried inside her body.

"That was—"

"Incredible," he finished.

Was it for him? He'd had more lovers than she had, by far. Hell, she could count hers on one hand and still have three fingers left over. But Blake, he'd have score sheets to compare notes. She wanted to ask, but her own insecurities stopped her.

"What's that look?" he asked, staring down at her face.

"What look?"

"The one of uncertainty, the one you have whenever you tell me you're too short or some such nonsense."

Theirs was a relationship based on honesty, but how much could she ask and not sound like a needy, emotional fool? "Was it? Incredible for you?"

"Samantha," he said on a breath. He lifted a hand to her face and stroked her chin with the back of his finger. His hips were still planted firmly against hers. "Do you notice how well your body fits against mine?"

Her breasts were flush with his chest, her legs wrapped around his hips. Their lips so close she could taste him still. "Yes."

"You're perfect. More passionate than I ever imagined. And although I'm beyond satisfied right now, I don't think I'm finished with you tonight. This"—he kissed her softly as he spoke—"is the start of a wonderful thing."

Well, he certainly knew how to make a woman smile even after her orgasm.

Blake unfolded from her arms long enough to stand. Then he picked her up and started walking from the room.

Samantha glanced at the floor with horror. "Blake, our clothes."

He chuckled. Ignoring her words, he carried her up the stairs to his room, where he made good on his earlier threat.

By the time she made it downstairs, it was late morning. Their clothes had been cleaned up, the dishes done. A picture of the two of them caught in the act of making love would have been the only thing plainer than the message they'd left for the staff to find. Her face heated with embarrassment, and she lowered her gaze every time she passed Mary or Louisa. The women were terribly polite. In fact, Samantha would have preferred they'd nudged her arm and given her a thumbs-up than act as if they cleaned up after Blake and his lovers every week.

As it was, Samantha broached the subject of previous lovers to Blake as they packed their clothes. "So, Blake," she started all innocent-like, "tell me, will I find any remnants of lovers past hidden in any of your dressers?"

He stopped and stood to stare at her, but she didn't skip a step while packing. After all, she was the one who needed to pack clothes. Blake had all he needed on two continents.

"I'm not sure what you mean."

"You know. Did Vanessa have a drawer of her own here, or Jacqueline?"

His stare bored holes into her back, but she refused to look him in the eye. She shouldn't care, but she wanted to know if he entertained his lovers in his home often.

"I never found anyone drawer-worthy," he told her.

Well, that was something. "Not even one panty left behind?"

She kept packing, not looking his way. *I'm pathetic.*

"Samantha?" He'd moved to stand behind her. His hands reached out and touched both her shoulders to turn her toward him. His gray eyes caught hers. "I've only had this home for four years. You're the only woman who's slept in my bed."

An inner smile blossomed deep in her chest, but she prevented it from spreading over her lips, not wanting him to see how much his words pleased her.

Samantha nodded.

He placed a soft kiss on her lips. "Would it bother you if there had been a drawer full of another woman's things?"

It shouldn't. Three weeks ago, they were

strangers. "Well, I guess not . . ." *Hell yes.*

"Samantha?" Her name was drawn out in a slow, knowing slide.

"OK, yes," she confessed. "Because . . ." She searched for a valid excuse and found one within easy reach. "Your staff will think better of me, or us . . . as a couple if I'm not just a number here at the house."

Pathetic. She shouldn't be trying to be more than a number. She should, however, be trying to build barriers around her heart, her feelings, and avoiding any emotional attachment to the man staring deep into her eyes.

"You're not a number, Samantha. If you ever feel like the staff here, or in Europe, are treating you otherwise, you need to let me know."

She shook her head. "Everyone's been wonderful."

Blake's eyes narrowed briefly, as if trying to solve a riddle. Then he turned away to finish his minimal packing.

When she turned back to her suitcase, she allowed a tiny smile to cross her lips. It was wrong of her to romanticize what was happening between them. They were only having a mutually satisfying sexual relationship and just happened to be married. No big deal.

"So, Samantha?" Blake forced his way into her thoughts.

"Yeah?"

"Have you ever had any drawer-worthy men in your life?"

Her hand hesitated. "No" was the short answer to her lack of a personal life.

They continued packing.

"Any recent boyfriends who might knock on the door?"

Samantha slid a glance over her shoulders. Blake had his back to her while he fiddled with something in his hand. OK, so her husband was curious about her past. It wasn't as if hers was splattered all over the tabloid news like his.

"The boyfriend well has been dry for some time," she offered.

"How dry?" he asked as the last word left her lips.

She turned and waited for him to feel her eyes and return her stare.

"When my father went to jail, I didn't allow myself to get close to anyone."

"You were twenty-one when your father was convicted."

"Right."

"There's been no one since—"

"None."

He pondered that for a minute, his gaze drifting toward the ceiling. "So that means—"

"I've had two lovers besides you," she gave him, knowing where this conversation was headed. It was strange knowing exactly what his

132

questions would be. "One in high school, because everyone goes to senior prom, and another in college." The one in college twisted her mind in two and ruined her trust in men.

There must have been something that crossed her face, because Blake dropped the questions and walked toward her again.

"Call it a male thing, but I like knowing I'm in a very exclusive list."

Thoughts of her college years, of the turmoil and pain, were hard to push from her mind. She forced a smile on her lips and a flip comment from her tongue. "Well, if a girl can't sleep with her husband, who can she sleep with?"

Blake's eyes narrowed. "Right."

He started to turn away, but a wedge had somehow formed between them. "Blake?"

"Yeah?"

"I like knowing I'm the only one who's been here."

Silence stretched before them. Both staring at each other and saying nothing. When Blake turned back to his task, Samantha finished hers.

Chapter Eight

The advantages to a private jet were sweeter with a woman. Making love midflight and finding a few hours of sleep should have left them both rested and relaxed as they made their descent. Sadly, he could sense Samantha's unease and did everything in his power to distract her.

He had booked a night at a hotel near the airport, with intentions of joining his family at Albany the following day. His family had other ideas.

When the jet landed in the early-morning hours, it was very late in the evening for Samantha and Blake. Blake could tell by the way Sam wrestled with her hands that her nerves were on high alert.

He kept his arm around her shoulders as they stepped out of the jet. At his suggestion, she'd slipped into a comfortable pair of worn jeans and a long-sleeve shirt. "No need to dress for the driver of the car," he'd told her, assuring her they would have time to sleep, shower, and dress properly before facing anyone of importance.

Yet when the car he'd ordered pulled up alongside the plane and the back door opened, his mother's high-heeled foot stopped both Blake and Samantha cold.

"You said we weren't expecting anyone at the airport," she hissed between thin lips.

"We aren't."

There was no denying his mother's frame as she slid from the backseat of the limousine. The driver held an umbrella over her head to keep the droplets of rain from ruining what a hairdresser had probably spent hours creating.

Despite her previous horrible marriage, Linda Harrison could have passed for a woman ten years her junior. Dark-umber hair was pulled gracefully back under a stylish hat. The long gray coat covered what Blake knew would be a slim-fitting skirt and blouse. His mother always dressed to perfection. Even though the sun was hidden under a thick layer of clouds, his mother wore a pair of large-rimmed sunglasses to hide her eyes and the feelings they might reveal.

"Then who's that?"

Blake swallowed. If there was one thing he'd learned about his wife, it was her insecurity. Despite all her shake-a-fist-at-you attitude, Samantha had an underlying desire to be accepted.

He knew, without a doubt, that his suggestion for her to change out of her silk pantsuit and into comfortable clothes was going to snap him in the ass later.

"That's my mother."

Sam's steps faltered, but Blake kept her moving with the steady pressure of his hand on her back.

"But—"

"Mum?" Blake removed his hand from Samantha's back long enough to kiss both his mother's cheeks. "We weren't expecting you." His tone was light, but he hoped he relayed his discontent.

"I couldn't let you and your bride arrive without a welcome."

Blake returned to Samantha's side and pushed her forward. "Samantha, my mother, Linda. Mum, I'd like you to meet my wife, Samantha."

His mother let a smile lift her lips. "A pleasure," she said, raising her hand to Samantha's.

"I've heard a lot about you."

"Is that so? I've heard nearly nothing about you."

Samantha stiffened beside him, and Blake quickly stepped between the two women. "We're here to fix that," he told his mother. "You didn't have to meet us here. You know how long the flight is from the States."

Linda patted Blake's shoulder. "I'm sure you've had plenty of time to rest in-flight."

"We've been very busy up until our trip, as I'm sure you can imagine. We're looking forward to a few hours' sleep."

His mother glanced at the driver holding the umbrella over her head and then to the car. "Then we should get you home to do so."

Blake felt his control starting to snap. The worst

part was that Samantha said absolutely nothing. She simply stared between the two of them, lips sealed.

"I've arranged a room at the Plaza."

"That's silly—"

"Mother!" He'd had enough.

"Linda? You don't mind if I call you Linda, do you?" Samantha found her voice.

"Of course not, dear."

"Good. As you can see, I'm in desperate need of a shower and some sleep. I hope you'll be so kind as to await our arrival at Albany, until Blake and I have had the opportunity to put some of that nasty jet lag behind us." Samantha's tone and words were more formal than Blake ever heard uttered previously from her lips.

"I suppose you are right."

Samantha grasped Blake's arm and leaned into him. "It really is nice of you to greet me here. You have no idea what that means to me."

Again, Blake was at a loss for words. He led his wife and mother into the back of the car and joined them.

The second the car door closed, Samantha snuggled closer to Blake's side. "That is a lovely coat," Sam told his mother.

"Th . . . Thank you."

"I hope you'll tell me where you got it. I'm afraid I've nothing like it, and from the looks of the sky, I'll need something like it for my trip."

"Of course. We'll have plenty of time to shop."

Blake's worry over his mother's untimely arrival started to fade. "My wife and my mother shopping. Should I be worried?" he teased.

"That depends," Samantha said.

"On?"

"If your sister joins us. Three women with an open credit card are positively dangerous."

They laughed. And despite the obvious differences between his mother and his wife, he wasn't worried about them getting along. Samantha had listened to his description about his mother's spending habits, about her love of fashion, and used it to gain her affection. By the time they reached the Plaza, Blake was certain his mother didn't even notice Samantha's department store jeans and nondesigner shoes. Blake was equally sure Samantha would burn the clothes on her back the minute she had a chance.

Thankfully, his mother waved them off at the door and didn't join them inside the hotel. The early-dawn hours graced them with a deserted lobby. The bellhop quickly shuffled them to their suite. Blake tipped the young man and closed the door behind him.

Alone, Sam toed off her shoes and flung herself on the sofa. "I might actually like your mom after I get over the fact she ambushed us at the airport."

"I asked her to wait for us in Albany."

"She's a mom. She's curious."

"Still, she should have waited." And he'd have a private word with her at the first opportunity.

"She needed to see that I wasn't five months pregnant with her own eyes."

Blake had started to place his suitcase on the bed when Samantha's words registered. "Pregnant?"

"Oh please, you didn't see her eyes drifting to my waist?"

No, the thought had never entered his mind. "You're not serious."

"Very. She was on a recon mission. First, to see if an heir is on the way; second, to make sure I wasn't a complete wash in the class department."

Blake leaned against the frame of the bed, his mind buzzing with the possibility that Samantha was right. "How can you be sure?"

"Women are emotional creatures. Everything is in their eyes. Once your mom took off her sunglasses, I could read every glance, every twitch."

He shrugged. "I think I need to have you come into my next management meeting. You seem to have the spy thing down."

"When I was in college, I minored in psychology."

"You could have had a career in criminal justice."

"Not likely. Sins of the father and all that."

Samantha pushed off the couch, ending their conversation. There was hurt in her stance as she unpacked a few things and headed for the bathroom. Her father had done a number on her. Sadly, Blake wasn't sure how deep her wounds were. He made a mental note to find out.

Samantha's head no sooner met the pillow than Blake was waking her. After a long, hot shower and a small meal—because face it, eating simply made her nauseous at this point—the honeymooners were on their way to Albany. The thought of Blake's family watching her every move spread shivers up her spine. Samantha knew she'd dodged Blake's mother's initial inquisition. There was no telling if Linda would be as easily put off once Sam was on the woman's home turf.

Dressed in a rust-colored skirt and dress jacket, she prepared herself to meet the family. Blake didn't even question why her jeans and shirt were dumped in the garbage can at the hotel. He simply noticed the outfit there and offered a laugh. Whatever! She shouldn't have brought it to begin with; then she wouldn't have been wearing it when Linda made her appearance. Not willing to be caught in anything but her best again, Samantha made certain the only clothes with her were on par with those of the former Duchess of Albany, maybe a few decades younger in style, but worthy of what the woman on Blake's arm should be wearing.

The rain let up during their afternoon drive to

the country. As London faded away, the rolling hills spread before them. She tried to relax in the seat beside Blake while he spoke of his sister, who was about Samantha's age.

"Gwen's always wanted me to settle down."

Sam felt her stomach twist with Blake's words. "Doesn't it worry you . . . ?" Sam let her words trail off, her gaze shifting to the driver in the front seat. She wanted to ask if he worried about his sister becoming attached to her new sister in the short span of their marriage.

Blake flinched. Uncertainty skirted over his face. "You and Gwen will get along fine. She's very kind. Perhaps a little spoiled, but never mean-spirited."

Samantha postponed her discussion about Gwen's attachment to a temporary sister-in-law for a time when the two of them could talk alone. The thought of deceiving all the people she was about to meet started to weigh on her. The memories of her father, of the time right before he was placed in handcuffs, surfaced in her mind.

As a business major, Samantha spent many hours outside class discussing her father's success with her professors. Even Dan, her boyfriend at the time, wanted to know everything about Harris Elliot and his small empire of wealth and property.

Dan had been charming, charismatic, and slier than a fox waiting at a hole for the rabbit to peek its soft, fuzzy head out.

Sam had been the rabbit who didn't know she was being played.

To think she'd slept with the man who eventually put her father behind bars. How stupid she'd been. They'd dated, studied, or so she thought, and rumpled a fair number of sheets. All the while Dan recorded their conversations, asked seemingly innocent questions, and helped the prosecution make their case against her father.

Even now, years later, sitting beside her temporary husband, Samantha felt ill at the thought. Not that she'd knowingly given the prosecution evidence against her father, but the sins of her father snowballed into the death of her mother and Jordan's wasted life.

Samantha remembered the day Dan had confronted her with the truth about who he was—how he'd stood beside a federal agent who threatened Samantha with her mother's incarceration if she didn't cooperate with their investigation. The agent and Dan revealed some of the holes in her father's business practices and informed her about the bugs throughout their home.

"We have reason to believe your mother knows more about your father's crimes. We need you to find proof otherwise, or we'll be forced to put them both behind bars."

Samantha knew her mother was clueless and was too shocked at the time to question why a federal agent would make a daughter prove a mother's innocence. In the end, Dan and his friends simply used Sam to nail her father. They knew her mother, Martha, had nothing to do with Harris's schemes.

Samantha had questioned many things her father did over the years. He had silent partners, or so he said, but Samantha never met one. It really wasn't until her first year in college, when her business professor asked about her father's profession, that Sam became suspicious. She couldn't give a concrete answer as to what her father did to make money—only that he did.

As for her mother, she was the wife of a rich man. She lunched with her elite neighbors, never washed her own dishes, and looked the other way when her father had an affair. Her clothes were always perfect, and she didn't allow Samantha or Jordan to leave the house in anything worn or cheap.

Samantha's first year in college opened her eyes to how the world really ran. Her sorority sisters, who disappeared like roaches to light when her father ended up in jail, showed Sam a lot about budgeting money. Two of the girls were from broken marriages and revealed their talents for skimming Daddy's money off their living expenses so they could take their spring breaks wherever the sisters wanted to go. They introduced Sam to big-box stores where everyday essentials didn't have to cost a small fortune. Samantha had been proud when she'd told her mom about how she'd budgeted her money so that her father's bill would be nearly half what they'd originally thought.

Martha took one look at the blue jeans Sam wore and refused to listen. "No daughter of mine is going to dress like that."

Offended, but not willing to let her mother's narrow mind stop her from learning financial reality, Samantha continued to put away nearly half of her father's allowance into a separate account every month. That account saved her ass when the Feds seized the Elliot money.

Now Samantha was shuffling right back into a lifestyle she'd left behind. She couldn't help worrying about how her deception to Linda, Gwen, and whomever else Blake introduced her to would turn out when Samantha and Blake split.

Blake's hand covered hers, bringing Sam's attention to the way she was twisting them in her lap. When she glanced into his beautiful gray eyes, she saw sympathy. *He probably thinks I'm nervous about meeting the family.*

Little could he know her worry went much deeper.

For the first time since she'd slid on his ring, she questioned her decision.

What if she said or did something to mess this

up for Blake, and his sister and mother were left without funds? Would Linda cope?

Sam shivered.

What if Linda took the path of Sam's mother?

Sam shook her head and forced away the memories of her mother's funeral.

"Everything is going to be fine."

Suddenly, Samantha wasn't so sure. Albany Hall unfolded in front of Samantha's eyes as the car drove up the secluded path to a circular drive.

"Oh my word," she hissed under her breath. Blake's childhood home was the size of a small castle. Two distinct wings jutted out from a central structure. Samantha counted three stories but didn't discard the fact there could be a massive basement belowground. According to Blake, there were thirty-five rooms, not including servants' quarters. Blake spoke of a ballroom and conservatory, a library with more volumes than anyone could ever possibly read, and sitting rooms aptly named by the color of the decor. "The Blue Room is off the main hall, the Red Room beside it."

Stepping out of the limousine and into Blake's world felt a bit like Cinderella at the ball. Only, the clock ticking would run for a year. Samantha should have felt comfortable with those thoughts, but she pictured the pumpkin, mice running at her feet, and her being left holding a glass slipper and regrets.

"Ready?" Blake asked before leading her inside.

• • •

If Gwen Harrison had any doubts about Samantha's presence beside Blake, she did a fine job of hiding it. She latched on to Sam's arm the minute Blake escorted her into the massive estate and didn't let go. She was young, beautiful, bubbly, and no doubt very spoiled. Linda greeted her with an easy smile and introduced Samantha to an aunt on Linda's side, Blake's uncle, and two cousins who both eyed her with speculation.

The servants stood ready to take her bags, bring her tea, and fade into the background.

"You can't know how pleased I am to have another woman close to my age around here," Gwen told Samantha. Where Blake hid his English accent, Gwen reveled in it.

"You've never lacked for company," Linda reminded her daughter.

"Company, yes, but with family, it's different. Wouldn't you agree, Samantha? I've never had a sister to confide in." Gwen flashed a beautiful white smile, and for a brief moment, Sam felt guilty. Although she had a sister, Jordan wasn't healthy enough to have a relationship with her like the one Gwen suggested.

It was as if Sam was being given a second chance at a sister through Blake. But again, that one-year time bomb on their relationship loomed. "I suppose," Samantha said.

"I have tea prepared in the Red Room, Blake. Why don't we sit in there so we can hear all about your whirlwind courtship and marriage?"

Blake managed to slide beside Samantha and take her arm. The heat of him by her side added some comfort to her wandering thoughts. He leaned next to her ear and whispered, "How are you doing?"

Samantha noticed Blake's cousin Howard watching them, his eyes narrowed, his lips pulled down. She lifted Blake's hand and kissed his knuckles. The light in her husband's face forced some of the foreboding of their future away. "Fine," she mouthed, and Blake squeezed her hand.

Linda ushered them into the Red Room with vaulted ceilings atop red, gray, and white wall-papered walls. The print was actually subtle despite the color. Floral paintings and silk drapes gave the room a feminine feel, and a lovely bouquet of fresh flowers sat on a mantel above a stone fireplace.

The men reached the spread of sweet cakes and finger sandwiches situated on the coffee table before they took tea.

"Have you been to Europe before?" Linda asked as she poured dark tea into tiny cups.

"When I was in high school."

"Then you know about teatime," Gwen said.

"It's just an excuse to snack midday," Blake told her.

Gwen waved her brother off. "Don't listen to him. He's allergic to anything remotely English. I don't think any of us were surprised to hear he'd taken an American wife."

"Gwen!" Linda scolded.

"It's true."

Samantha chuckled.

"It isn't my fault the women in Europe didn't hold my interest," Blake defended himself.

Howard stopped eating to ask, "So you and Samantha have known each other for a long time?"

Samantha and Blake agreed that he would be the one to field questions about their relationship. That way, neither of them could stumble over the other.

"I wouldn't say that."

"What would you say?" Mary, Blake's aunt, asked.

"We met last month."

"Last month?" Gwen sounded shocked. "How can you marry someone you hardly know?"

Blake put his tea down and reached for Samantha's hand. "I would have married Samantha on the first day had she said yes. There are some things in life you just know are the right thing to do."

Paul, Blake's uncle, sat forward in his chair. "The right thing, you say. Is there something you're not telling us?"

Blake's jaw tightened. "What are you asking?"

The women fell silent, their eyes on Samantha. "Is she pregnant?"

Blake stiffened. "She has a name, and I insist you start using it instead of acting like Samantha isn't in the room." The deadly delivery of Blake's words chilled her. This was a side of him she hadn't seen often and hoped to never see from the receiving end.

A smug smile crossed Paul's face, but before he could say anything else, Samantha answered, "I'm not pregnant."

Even though the women in the room had said nothing, there was a collective sigh between them with the announcement.

"Then you married because of the will." This had come from Adam, the youngest cousin sitting beside Howard, who said nothing.

Blake was on his feet, fists clenched.

Samantha scrambled to set her tea aside and grasped Blake's hand. "Darling, we knew they'd question our motives." Then, as if she were born to lie, she said, "How could they possibly know the energy that passed between us that first day we met or understand our motives to be together and married without a long courtship?"

Linda finally spoke up, putting some ease in the room. "You make it sound so romantic, Samantha."

Sam pulled Blake back into his chair and latched on to his hand to keep him from wringing the necks of the men in the room. "I'm sure you don't want all the details, but your son is very romantic."

"I want the details." Gwen bit her lip as she spoke.

Blake's eyes narrowed at his sister.

Samantha's gaze skirted toward Howard. The man watched the entire scene without saying a word. His silence told her he didn't approve. His cold stare reached toward Blake, and Samantha couldn't help but wonder how far Howard would go to get his hands on Blake's inheritance.

The older Parker, of Parker and Parker, sat opposite Blake in his office to discuss a few particulars of his father's last will and testament. Blake remembered hearing his father's proclamation from the grave demanding that he marry in order to inherit the bulk of his wealth, but he'd missed some of the details. Actually, Blake had cut the lawyer off at the time. Blake had just turned thirty when his father died. Thirty-six seemed a long way off.

Wearing a suit, tie, and a stoic expression, Mark Parker opened his briefcase and removed a stack of papers two inches thick. "I see you wasted little time securing a wife," the man said. The last meeting between the two of them had been only two months ago. Mark reminded Blake of the deadline Edmund had mapped out, but did so only because he was obligated to. Had Blake missed the deadline, Parker and Parker would stand to gain twenty-five percent of the estate, his sister and mother would be given a small stipend, although not enough to maintain their current lifestyle, and the rest would go to Howard and a few charities.

"Samantha and I are very happy," Blake told the man, offering no apologies.

"Is that so?"

"I'm sure you'll see for yourself this weekend. I haven't looked forward to going home at the end of my day in some time." Funny, the words didn't feel like a lie as they left his tongue. He did in fact look forward to seeing Samantha every night and every morning since they'd started to share a bed.

Mark's lips pinched together, the crow's-feet along his eyes became more defined. "Convincing the firm that your marriage isn't one of convenience will fall on you and *your wife*."

"I'm well aware of the stipulations Edmund put in his will. We're here today to outline exactly what your firm needs from me over the next twelve months."

Mark scraped his fingers over his jaw. "Your father was determined to see to it that you do more than manipulate your way through his demands."

His father was an ass. But there was no need to

tell Mark his thoughts on the dead man now. "We already know that."

"He spent a considerable amount of time in our offices writing up legal contingencies."

Something in the way Mark was sitting up, how the man's eyes had a certain spark, brought the hair on Blake's arms to stand on end. "We've gone over those contingencies."

Mark's mouth opened into a silent *O* before he cocked his head to the side and said, "Most of them. We've discussed most of them."

The floor under Blake started to drop. Instead of showing the sly lawyer his unease, Blake sat back in his chair and waited for the other man to elaborate.

"I'm sure, at the time of the reading of Edmund's will, you were too upset to listen to a few incidentals. Like the one where once you were married, a codicil he had added was to be read and followed." Mark was smiling now, like a fox staring down at a mouse.

"I'm intrigued," Blake uttered. "What else could my father possibly ask for?"

"Here is a sealed addendum that was to be opened after you married." After removing a set of papers from the pile, he started to read. *"Good show, Blake, my boy, seems I didn't raise a complete fool, after all. By now, I'm sure to have made your list of the worst humans who've ever roamed this earth. I assure you, my intentions are only to prove to you once and for all how important your family should be to you. You mocked me most of your adult life, did everything in your power to put stress in mine. I suppose a better man would have died comfortable that he'd left his children and wife well provided for instead of forcing his heir to his will. We both know I wasn't that man. So, my son, I leave you with one final demand before your inheritance is turned over to you. I trust that you've married just prior to your thirty-fifth birthday, which gives you one year to accomplish your next task.*

The blood in Blake's veins started to boil, knowing damn well where his father was going, yet not being able to stop the words from leaving Mark Parker's mouth.

"If you're truly settled down and ready to continue my family line, then the proof will come by way of an heir."

Mark paused to assess Blake's reaction.

Blake forced his jaw to remain loose, his hands folded in his lap. The image of Samantha swam in his head.

What was he going to do now?

"These things take time, but within a year, you should be well on your way to becoming a father."

Like before, Blake stopped listening when Mark went on about the sex of the child not making a difference, and that the child need not be born before Blake's thirty-sixth birthday. Mark finished speaking and cleared his throat. "Seems your father thought of everything."

"And if my wife and I wanted to wait to start a family?"

Mark huffed. "Your father is giving you millions of reasons to push your plans forward. Of course, if you weren't planning on a family or planning on staying married to—"

Blake put his hand in the air, interrupting the lawyer's words. "We're newlyweds, Mark. Or perhaps that's escaped your attention."

"Nothing you're doing escapes my attention. Bigger men than you have married to get their hands on large amounts of money, with no intentions of staying married after their funds are in the bank." Mark was angry now, his words short with his crisp accent.

"This addendum was sealed, but you knew about it all along, didn't you?"

Mark sat back in his chair and crossed his arms over his chest. The slight lift of his lips gave Blake his answer.

Blake had an uncharacteristic desire to make Mark, and all his callousness, squirm in his chair. "I rather like the thought of being a father," Blake said, letting a little of his childhood accent dip into his words.

Mark's smile fell.

"Samantha will make a lovely mother." Which Blake really did believe. He kept his poker face fully engaged.

"It's going to take more than words to convince us."

"Of that, I have no doubt."

Mark gathered his papers and stood to leave. "I'll be in touch."

Blake stood and extended his hand. "We'll see you this weekend at the reception."

"Right."

As the lawyer turned to leave, Blake stopped him. "Oh, Mark, be sure and have your secretary make me a copy of my father's will."

Mark nodded and left Blake's office.

Turning on his heel, Blake walked to the office window to stare across the rain-soaked streets.

A baby.

Damn his father and everything the man stood for. Part of Blake wanted to walk away. Tell Samantha their bluff had been called. He knew damn well Samantha wouldn't be willing to bring a child into this world for the sake of millions. Her family and their deception had already caused her too much trauma. She wouldn't deceive a child. Hell, Blake could practically feel the twisting in Samantha's gut when Gwen started talking about plans for the future.

Blake had anticipated the lawyers at Parker and Parker would try to force him and Samantha together over the course of the next year. He'd thought Mark was in his office today to say something to the effect of, *Blake, old boy, you and your wife cannot be apart any more than two weeks at a time for the firm to believe you are happily married.*

No, the law firm had done something much more difficult to produce.

But what if Samantha did end up pregnant? Would that be so bad? A warmth starting low in his belly rose through his chest. The thought of her curves rounding out, the swell of her breasts filling his palm even more than they already did, her holding out a son for him to claim . . .

Blake shook the images, which weren't that hard to picture, from his mind.

Maybe his own legal team could find something illegal about his father's will. He'd put the best on the case to see what could be done.

In the meantime, he'd keep the latest twist in his life to himself.

Chapter Nine

Samantha was having a hell of a time shaking the jet lag, and they'd been in Europe for over a week. Then again, living a lie was exhausting. Even Blake seemed stressed around the edges.

The reception was the next day, and everything was set to go. What Samantha needed was time away from Blake's demanding family. She'd escaped into the library, determined to find a diversion, when Blake found her.

"There you are."

Blake looked good enough to eat, wearing casual slacks and a pullover sweater that emphasized his broad shoulders.

"I thought you went to the office."

He shook his head. "I couldn't leave you today."

Confused, she asked, "What's so special about today?"

He brought a hand to his chest and faked a mortal wound. "I can't believe you've forgotten."

Samantha laughed. "Don't give up your day job for that acting gig," she teased.

"You really don't know what today is, do you?"

It wasn't a holiday, English or American, his birthday had already passed, and hers wasn't for a few months. "Nope, color me clueless."

Blake took her hands in his and brought her

up against his chest. "We've been married one month."

Oh Lord, he was right. The fact that he'd thought of it and was making a big deal over it showed just how much of a sentimental sap the dashing duke was. "Wow. A whole month already." It felt so much longer.

"I know how to celebrate it too."

"You want to celebrate our one-month anniversary?" Samantha glanced around Blake's shoulder to see if anyone was nearby and listening. She couldn't see into the hallway, so she kept her questions as to why the big deal to herself.

Blake winked at her and laced his fingers with hers. "Come on."

He tugged her from the room, down the massive hall, and out the front door. "Where are we going?" This was a carefree Blake she liked seeing.

"Away."

"Cryptic much?" she asked. "Where?"

"You'll see."

Instead of leading her to a car, he walked her down to the stables. "You said you rode, right?"

They'd had the conversation about horses after they'd arrived at Albany. "I do, but it's been a long time."

"Where we're going isn't far."

The sun was making a rare appearance. The warm air and birds flying around helped lift the stress from Samantha's shoulders. At the stable, two horses were saddled and ready. Blake thanked the young man who'd readied their mounts and then whispered something into the kid's ear that Samantha couldn't hear.

The boy blushed, sent Samantha a quick glance, and then turned away. "Yes, sir," he told Blake.

"Need a hand getting on?" Blake asked her.

The chestnut horse eyed her suspiciously as she approached. After a couple of pets, the mare managed a snort, as if to say, *Whatever*.

"I might need a leg up."

Blake cupped his hands for her to use as leverage. After a couple of tries, she was on the back of the horse with reins in hand.

Like a seasoned rider, Blake mounted in one clean swoop, his back rod-straight as he led them from the stable and out into the fresh air.

"So, what is this horse's name?" Samantha asked as they led the horses across the wide-open space behind Albany Hall.

"I think it's Maggie."

"And yours?"

"Blaze."

Tilting her head back, Samantha laughed. "Maggie sounds slow, and Blaze sounds fast."

Blake winked at her. "Exactly."

"I told you I knew how to ride. No need to put me on the grandmother in the barn." Maggie tossed her head back, causing both Blake and Samantha to chuckle.

"I don't think she liked that," he suggested. "You told me you hadn't ridden in quite a while. I wouldn't want to be responsible for a broken anything if you're thrown."

Sam stretched over the neck of her horse and patted the coat behind Maggie's ear. "You won't throw me, will you?"

"She wouldn't dare."

Samantha considered kicking the horse into something faster than a walk but didn't have any idea where they were headed.

"When was the last time you rode?" Blake asked.

"Before . . ." She let the word hang there for a moment, as if Blake would know its meaning. For many years, everything in her life was either before the fall of her family or after.

Samantha noticed Blake watching her patiently. "Before my father went to prison. Before my mother's death. Before Dan. Before Jordan's suicide attempt. Jordan and I used to ride all the time." The memory of her sister on a horse made her smile.

"Who's Dan?"

Had she said his name? "Dan was the snake I dated in college."

"There's a story behind that."

Blake didn't press her for answers. Maybe that was why she didn't have a problem opening up to him. "Dan dated me to learn more about my father. He worked for the Feds."

Blake's expression turned to stone. "He slept with you to get to your dad?"

The anger in his voice put a smile on her face. It was so nice to have someone see it her way. "Slept with me. Told me he loved me. Women aren't the only ones who lie to get what they want."

"That must have hurt."

She remembered those days, the pain, the deception. "I guess you know now why I have a hard time trusting people."

"I should be honored that you trust me."

"Damn right." She laughed and sent him a wink. They weren't out on this beautiful day to walk through her past.

Blake brought his horse closer to hers, reached for her hand, and brought the back of it to his lips for a small kiss.

Her heart lunged in her chest and cracked wide open. Try as she might, she couldn't help but compare her feelings for him to the man she once claimed to love. The two didn't belong on the same planet.

"Where are you taking me?" she asked, changing the subject.

Blake slid a glance over his shoulder, a smirk playing on his lips. "You don't do surprises very well, do you?"

"I do. It's just . . . OK, no, I don't do surprises. Where are we going?"

Blake pointed to a patch of trees about a mile away. "There's a cottage by a stream where I thought we'd enjoy a quiet lunch."

Samantha allowed her shoulders to slump and a silly grin to grace her lips. "That's sweet."

"That's me, Mr. Sweet."

He was being sarcastic, but she thought the title worked. "Just beyond those trees, huh?"

"Yep." He kept his horse at a walk. His thighs hugged the flanks of the animal he rode and drew Samantha's gaze to him once again. Blake's strong profile and broad shoulders that tapered to his perfect behind made her mouth water. The thought of the cottage, with privacy, popped into her mind.

"How long will it take us to get there?"

"Half an hour at most."

"Hmmm." Then, without warning, Samantha kicked Maggie and held on as the horse lurched ahead.

"Sam?" Blake was calling her name from behind her.

She fixed her knees into the horse and held on tight until Maggie had found a nice comfortable pace for her run.

Hardly a few seconds passed before Blake overtook her. The frown on his face dissipated when he saw her smile as he passed. Instead of forcing them to a stop, he let Blaze take the lead, and Maggie followed.

Cool air coursed through Samantha's hair, pulling it out of the clip she'd used to hold it back. The landscape buzzed past, but not so quickly that she missed the scent of lavender blooming or fresh grass under the horses' hooves. This she could get used to. The freedom of riding away from life's worries, the big outdoors to escape into.

They cleared the open space in five minutes and had to slow the horses to pick their way through the trees. Seemed both Maggie and Samantha were in need of catching their breath. "That was wonderful."

Blake's gray eyes caught hers and held. For the second time that day, he looked relaxed and carefree. For a moment, she thought he was going to say something, but he lowered his eyes and pulled on the reins to move Blaze deeper into the woods.

"It's so beautiful here. And quiet."

"When I was a kid, I used to take a horse out here all the time to escape my father."

"Was he so bad?" Seemed her husband and his father had the worst of relationships, but Blake hadn't really elaborated.

"I wasn't him."

"And that's what he wanted, a miniature him?"

Blake nodded.

Samantha wanted to ask more questions, but Blake moved his horse in front of hers as the path narrowed. Soon the sound of water sounded over the horses.

When the trees opened up to reveal the stream, Samantha knew why Blake had chosen this place as a getaway. Crystal-clear water cascaded down rocks and dipped around fallen branches and trees. Moss and grass grew along the banks of the stream. It made her envision Blake as a little boy sitting by the water's edge tossing rocks.

"Is this still on your land?"

"It is. The estate is over five hundred acres. But this is the most beautiful location on it."

"It's amazing, Blake."

The path opened to a small meadow with a cottage sitting on one end. Once they cleared the trees, Blake swung off his horse. "We'll let them drink before we hitch them."

Samantha slid to the ground with wobbly legs. But the energy felt good, refreshing. As the horses drank from the stream, she asked, "How often is this cottage used?"

"Not often. For a time, I was the only one who came out here. I think Gwen used to escape here after I moved away."

"I'll have to ask her."

Blake led the horses to a post and tied them with enough rope to allow them to graze. "Let me show you inside."

Samantha took his hand, enjoying the warmth

of his fingers circling hers, and walked beside him up the few steps to the cabin porch.

The door swung open with a tiny nudge. "You don't lock it?"

"No need."

As she stepped inside, Samantha's breath caught in her throat.

In the center of the room was a table set for two. Linen napkins, beautiful china, and crystal goblets were waiting for them to enjoy. A bucket stood to the side with wine chilling inside. Large silver trays were covered with food. "Oh, Blake, this is lovely."

"You like?"

She turned to him and wove a hand around his waist. Looking up into his eyes, she smiled and tipped her lips to his. "I love it."

Blake accepted her lips for a brief kiss, but when she started to pull away, he held her close and moved his head to the side. Her kiss of gratitude swiftly moved from a thank-you to more.

The feel of his hands roaming down her back brought a moan from deep inside her chest. Everywhere he touched heated instantly. Whenever they made love, it seemed they couldn't touch enough. Blake nibbled at her lip as his hand reached for her breast. "I'm an awful person," he said between kisses.

Her head fell back, already lost. "Why do you say that?"

He backed her into the room and kicked the door closed behind them. "We haven't even eaten, and I'm already crawling all over you."

Laughing, she kicked her shoes free and peeled away at his sweater. "Are you saying we were only supposed to eat?"

Blake helped her with his shirt by flinging it across the room. "Eat first, then make love. That was the plan."

Licking her way across his collarbone and down to one taut nipple, she laughed. "Make love, then eat"—she nibbled a path to his other side—"then make love again."

Tugging her clothes free, Blake kept backing her away from the food to the only bedroom in the cottage. Samantha hardly glimpsed the lace curtains framing the window or the patterned quilt covering the mattress before Blake pressed her under him.

"You feel so good," she told him, loving the weight of him on top of her.

"Yes, you do." His fingers managed to unclasp her bra and toss it aside in seconds. His lips claimed her nipple as he laved up one side, circled her dusky tip, and nipped. "Tastes like spring," he whispered before shifting his attention to the other side. He took his time with slow, even strokes of his tongue. Samantha writhed with pleasure. Traveling down her tight stomach, he peeled away her pants, kissing a path over her hip and down her thigh.

They always gave in to the need for penetration when they'd made love, but already, Samantha felt this time would be different, slower, and just as satisfying. The soft pad of Blake's thumb traced up her thighs after her pants were on the floor. He hooked a finger under her panties and petted the sensitive skin at her hip.

"I think," he said, blowing a heated breath above her flesh, "that my nourishment will come before and after we eat what's in the other room."

A tinge of vulnerability shot through her. For all her talk and ease with Blake in the bedroom, having a man kiss the sensitive flesh between her legs wasn't something she'd experienced before.

"What is it?" Blake asked, his chin dangerously close to her damp panties, his eyes narrowed in concern.

"I . . . I've not." Darn, she wasn't a virgin, but in this, she was. "No one has ever . . ." She let her gaze drift to her mound before returning to him.

Recognition flecked in his eyes, and a soft smile spread over his lips. "Never?"

She gave a quick shake of her head.

He lowered his lips to kiss the skin below her belly button, his eyes never leaving hers. "I like that."

With his three simple words, she let the vulnerability go and relaxed into Blake's masterful arms. His tongue sought her flesh as he removed the scrap of material between her thighs. He

167

pressed hot, open-mouthed kisses around her core until her thighs opened to give him room. Blake kissed, licked, and moaned over her until her will nearly snapped with the want of more. When his lips connected with the most sensitive spot on her body, Samantha nearly leapt from the bed. Blake kept her anchored, his tongue swirling around her, chasing and coaxing tiny building spasms deep inside her body. The intensity of her pending release was like nothing she'd experienced before. He took her to the edge, drew back, and had her clutching his shoulders tight.

He was teasing her, teaching her to crave this from him, and all she could do was beg for more. "Please."

With a flick of his tongue and a gentle suck, Samantha welled over and cried out her release. Her body trembled as she rode the sensation to the very end.

When Samantha felt it was safe to open he eyes, she found Blake smiling over her. His broad hands ran the length of her body as he waited for her attention.

"You're sinful," she uttered, her voice low and throaty.

He placed a delicate kiss on her lips. "You're sexy. Now that I've tasted you, I'm going to want more."

Her hand feathered over his hip, surprised to see he'd managed to free himself of his clothes. Not being of a mind to take and not give in return, Samantha offered a grin before pushing Blake on his back to have a taste of him. Following his example, she traced his hip, first with her fingers, then with her tongue. The salty musk of his skin tantalized her taste buds until her mouth watered.

"Should I be worried?" he hissed as she let her cheek graze his erection.

"What?" she asked, pretending innocence with her tone. "I've seen movies." She hadn't, but she wanted to keep him guessing. In this, she had a brief encounter. Then there were the books she'd read once in a while. Seems tons of authors must have some idea how this worked.

"But—"

Samantha drew him into the deep, warm cavern of her mouth.

"Sweet Lord." Blake moaned, his hips tilting forward, asking for more.

Samantha smiled over him, lapping, tasting, and desiring his pleasure nearly as much as her own. The musky scent of his skin and sex filled her as she brought him to the very edge of release before pulling back. She would have continued, but Blake gently forced her away. "Too much."

"You don't like?" she teased, knowing he more than liked what she was doing. She wanted to finish him as he'd done to her.

"Another time," he said, before reaching for his wallet and removing a condom.

Samantha helped him with the thin latex and then crawled over his body. She kissed him fully on the mouth, their tastes mingling as he pressed inside her. Slick with desire, he filled every inch of her, stretching her. Blake rose to meet her body, retreated, and plunged again. His fingers tangled with her hair and held on tightly as her body responded to his with renewed passion and need.

Samantha couldn't get enough of him. Her breasts scraped against the soft dusting of hair on his chest. His heartbeat pressed past his ribs and into hers. As much as she told herself their time together was for physical release, for a mutually satisfying sexual experience, tiny slivers of her heart melted into his.

They moved together, straining like strings of a violin, until she unwound and shattered. Muscles strained on Blake's arms as he held her close and moaned his release into her ear.

As the world stilled and Blake murmured tender words, Samantha knew she was in trouble. Falling in love with her husband was not part of their plan. In spite of the honesty they had in their relationship, voicing her concerns didn't seem wise.

As their breath slowed and the heat from their bodies drifted into the air, Samantha forced herself away from his arms. Her stomach growled at that very moment, giving her the perfect escape. "I'm starving."

• • •

Albany Hall filled with people, all wanting to get a glimpse of the new duchess, the woman Blake had finally married. People would whisper—that Blake had expected—but none would dare show anything but respect to him and his bride.

Blake caught Samantha at the far end of the room, talking with Gwen and the couple standing beside her. Samantha wore a stunning ivory silk evening gown that dipped to the small of her graceful back. He'd placed an emerald pendant around her neck, with matching earrings to adorn her ears. The four-inch heels peeked out from under the silk through a slit that went the length of her thigh. His wife was magnificent. Poised with elegance that couldn't be taught and beauty that wasn't skin deep. Blake felt truly proud to call her his wife.

Carter, who had flown in for the reception, stood by his side. "I can't get over the transformation of your wife," he whispered so only Blake could hear.

"She is beautiful." Funny, Blake wasn't surprised with the changes. Samantha seemed to be blossoming before his eyes, every day a little more light shone in her eyes, a little more confidence shone in her steps.

"It's more than that." Carter's gaze cut away to one of the Parker lawyers across the room. "How is everything else going?"

Blake wasn't about to talk about any details

with a roomful of ears. "Perfectly. We'll be going back to the States in a few days. Gwen wanted to come back with us, but I convinced her that Samantha and I need some time alone before we start entertaining family."

Carter laughed. "Did that work?"

"Of course." Why wouldn't it? Half the family had noticed them arrive from their ride to the cottage the previous day. After making love, eating lunch, then finding a sunny spot of grass to make love a second time, their clothes and hair were rumpled and a mess. There was no mistaking their actions.

"Careful, Blake."

Blake lifted his glass with his drink in his hand and stared over the rim at his friend. "Careful about what?"

"Something about you feels different. Be careful."

Blake squared his shoulders. "I'm always careful."

Samantha walked toward them, a smile on her lips.

Blake set down his glass and slid an arm around her waist. "You remember Carter?"

"How can anyone forget Carter?" Samantha leaned forward when Carter kissed her cheek. Although his best friend didn't threaten him in the least, Blake didn't like seeing her eyes light up when they looked at his friend. "Is Hollywood calling you yet?"

Carter laughed. Samantha had made a joke about his Hollywood good looks landing him a job on a movie set if he ever got tired of pursuing a career as a politician.

"Not yet. I'm still waiting, though."

Blake's arm tightened around her frame.

"Your mother suggested we move into the ballroom to start the dancing. Seems no one will begin until we spin around a couple of times."

The thought of Samantha pressing close to him motivated his feet. "If you'll excuse us."

Carter nodded as they walked away.

"Have I told you how lovely you are tonight?" Blake whispered close to her ear.

"You did. You clean up well yourself."

Enjoying her compliment, Blake smiled. He wore a tux, and why not? They didn't have the opportunity to dress for their wedding, so this would have to do.

They entered the ballroom, where a string quartet played in one corner. When they spotted the two of them, they ended the song they were playing and started another.

The moment the music began, he led Samantha to the center of the room and swung her into his arms. Her hands lifted to his shoulders as they swayed to the music. Samantha's cheeks blossomed with color. "People are staring."

Blake fanned his fingers along the edge of her dress to the small of her back and pressed her close. "That's what they do for the bride and groom's first dance." And because he felt her stiffen, he teased her. "They want to see me trip." Blake spun her around, their bodies close.

"They might be waiting for a while; you seem to know what you're doing out here."

Blake removed one of her arms from his neck and led her into another swing before bringing her back. "I've danced a time or two."

"Or three or four."

She followed his lead, easing into his arms. By the time the dance ended, he was staring into her eyes. He lowered his lips to hers for a small taste.

Cameras flashed and several people clapped as the quartet picked up another song. This time the dance floor started to fill.

Samantha lifted her lips to his ear. "Was that kiss for the cameras?"

His lips lifted. "That kiss was for you. But this one"—he dipped her low, arching her back and taking her mouth to his again before bringing her back up—"is for the cameras."

Samantha chewed on her bottom lip as she smiled. "Jeez, and I thought the English frowned on such public displays of affection."

Blake tossed his head back with laughter. "And we both know how much I long to be English."

Laughing, they spun around until Blake felt someone tap his shoulder. He twisted to see Carter grinning. "Mind if I cut in?"

Blake almost told him to bugger off. Instead, he tilted his head to his bride and let Carter dance with her.

His gaze followed them around the dance floor, wondering what Carter was saying to make her laugh.

"Easy, big brother," Gwen cooed beside him. "They're just dancing."

"What?" Blake blinked and looked down at his sister.

"Dancing? I was hoping you'd dance with me." She tugged on his hand until he conceded. "I really like her."

Blake had to spin Gwen to see his wife. "She likes you too."

"She's a lot nicer than any of the girls you've been dating. I can see why you married her. Not to mention she's American, which Dad would have hated."

Blake forced his attention to his sister and her words. "I didn't marry her to spite our dead father." No, he'd married her because of his dead father.

"But it doesn't hurt that he wouldn't have approved."

Was he so transparent that even his sister could see his demons? What if he was going through all this effort, all the lies, to tick off a dead man? What happened when Blake let go of all the animosity and pain from his past?

"Don't frown, Blake. People will think we're fighting."

Blake turned to his sister and forced a smile to his face. "What about you, Gwendolyn, had you ever thought of going against the man?"

"No." She shook her head. "Mother needed me here. Can you imagine being left with him by yourself?"

Blake actually blinked with his sister's words. "I can't, but I don't think our mother would want you to give up your life for her."

Gwen patted his arm. "I know. We've talked about me traveling, seeing more of the world without her by my side. I suppose, now that you've settled down, Mother will focus more on you and your family."

"It's just Samantha and me."

"Please, I have eyes. It won't be long before there are more of you."

The song was fading to a close and, luckily, the end of their dance. "We haven't even cut the wedding cake, Gwen. Let's not start talking about birthday cakes."

But his mind was already there, had been ever since Mark polluted his plans with another block.

He and Gwen parted, and Blake turned to search Samantha out. Unfortunately, his aunt cornered him for a dance, and Samantha was already in the arms of one of his sly cousins.

The party went into the early-morning hours.

Out-of-town guests stayed in several rooms at the estate, while those who lived locally went home.

Back in their room, Samantha removed her heels at the door and sank into the carpet with her toes. "Oh, that feels good."

"I didn't think some of the guests would ever leave."

"Leave? Some of the men retired to the Blue Room for cards and cigars. You'd think they were English gentleman of the eighteenth century the way they spoke."

Blake loosened his tie and toed off his shoes. "What do you mean?"

"One guy, I think his name was Gilbert—"

"Gilabert," he corrected, instantly picturing the man in his head. "Old money like his father, with his ways set in stone."

"Silly name for a grown man, but whatever. Gilabert waved off one of his poker friend's wives when she asked if she could join them for a game. 'Oh, no. Ladies aren't allowed.'" Samantha had dipped her voice low and forced an English slant to her tongue.

"That sounds like him."

"If he'd said that to me, I'd have sat at the man's right-hand side just to annoy him."

Blake would like to see that. "Imagine that tenfold, and you may be able to picture my father."

Samantha stared, horrified. "I'm so sorry."

"Me too."

Shaking her head, she stepped into the walk-in closet, and Blake started to pull his shirt from his pants.

"We're a mess, you and I," Samantha said from the other room.

"Really? Why's that?"

"Our dads did a number on us. Yours is reaching from the grave, still calling the shots, and mine had me questioning every man who ever walked into my life."

Blake flung his shirt to the back of a chair before unzipping his pants. "You don't seem to question me."

"Oh, I did, in the beginning—those first few days, anyway. But you've grown on me."

He smiled at the thought. "Really?"

"You've been nothing but honest from the beginning. I admire that."

He hesitated. He should say something now, about the tiny new problem the lawyer had brought up. But Blake's mouth went as dry as a desert.

"I was shocked when some of your colleagues told me how ruthless you are in business. I guess I've not seen that side of you."

He was all that and more. Blake didn't lose. His eye never left the goal until it was met. "Was someone bad-mouthing me?"

"Oh please, Blake. Like I would have allowed that. No, not bad-mouthing. Just informing me. It was strange, even the lawyer . . . What was his name?"

Blake's heart slammed into his chest. "Mark Parker?"

"That's it."

He had to sit down. Good thing the bed was at his back.

"He said your father and you held the same merciless way of getting what you want. I had to laugh. I kept thinking of you sitting at the restaurant in Malibu telling me everyone had a price. Mark seemed like he wanted to add something, but I kept giggling. I think he got irritated with me before walking away."

A long-winded sigh hissed from Blake's lips. Mark had kept his mouth shut. Thank God.

It wasn't as if Blake would keep the new portion of the will from Samantha forever, just that he needed more time to find a loophole, something, so that he could keep his inheritance and Samantha.

Well, for a year, anyway.

Less than twelve months.

Samantha cleared her throat from across the room, where she stood leaning against the door-frame.

She'd slipped into a white lace teddy with barely there panties that covered nearly nothing. Her hair that had been piled high all night fell to her shoulders in a beautiful auburn cloud.

In her hand was an empty condom box. "Please

tell me you have more of these?" She waved the box in a circle.

"And here I expected you to be too tired tonight." Him too, for that matter. But his body sprang to life as she walked toward him, her hips swaying in time to the beat of his heart.

He had stripped to his boxers, and Samantha's gaze shifted low. "You're not tired."

She slid a hand up his chest. He sucked in the scent of her skin. Three hundred and sixty-five days didn't seem to be enough.

"Besides," she whispered in her deep, sexy bedroom voice. "We didn't celebrate our real wedding night the way we should have. I think we need to make up for lost time." She tapped the box against his chest. "But we need more of these. When I get back to the States, I'll see a doctor, but until then, we need to be careful."

"My suitcase," he told her. "I'll get them." He didn't want to be tempted to take what she didn't freely give, so he walked away and found a half-empty box of contraceptives.

When he returned to his bed, Samantha was already spread over the covers, one knee pulled up in offering. Blake forced away thoughts of lawyers, tomorrow, and a year from now while he made love to his wife.

Chapter Ten

After returning to the States, Sam immediately drove to Moonlight to visit Jordan. Guilt over enjoying her time in Europe with Gwen, coupled with the excitement over her new life with Blake, knotted her stomach when she walked into Jordan's room. Her sister's strawberry-blonde hair was tied back with a scrunchie, and her pink cotton shirt sported a stain where some of her lunch had missed the mark.

"Hey, hon," Samantha said as she moved to a chair across from where Jordan stared out the window.

Jordan offered a half smile, all she could manage after the stroke. Her eyes lit up with recognition, and she lifted her good arm, which Samantha grasped in a tight grip.

"M . . . Miss you." Jordan's words were slurred.

"I missed you too." She'd only missed one scheduled visit, but Samantha knew Jordan looked forward to them. It wasn't like her baby sister had a lot in life to pull her out of bed in the morning. "Have you been eating?"

"Yes," she said with her mouth, but her head shook in denial. One of the things that Samantha had learned to do was to read Jordan's body language more than her words. The words didn't come easy and often didn't match Jordan's thoughts. Facial expressions and gestures were the key to understanding her.

"Do you want to help me with some of this Mongolian beef? It's from the Golden Wok, your favorite place."

Jordan smiled. "I like there."

"I know. Me too." Samantha opened a box of takeout, and the scent of spicy beef spilled into the air. After fixing a rolling tray in front of her sister and a small plate of food, Samantha pressed a fork into Jordan's hand. Jordan hated to be fed. Even though her sister struggled to get the food in her mouth, she wasn't happy if she didn't do it on her own.

"I . . . I seen . . . um . . . I see . . ." Jordan struggled to find the words.

"You saw who?" Samantha bit into her late lunch, realizing for the first time that she hadn't eaten all day. She and Blake had arrived late the previous evening and slept in. Before lunch, they'd both gone their separate ways—Blake to the office, Samantha to see Jordan. Food hadn't even crossed her mind. The tantalizing flavors exploded in her mouth, and her stomach rumbled with appreciation.

"Mom."

Samantha's fork stalled.

Jordan nodded.

Samantha placed her fork down. "Honey, Mom's been gone for a long time."

Jordan's brow pitched together, as if searching for a memory. "At night. Seen her at night."

"In a dream?"

"Yes." Jordan shook her head. "At night."

Now Samantha was confused. Did Jordan see someone who looked like their mother? Maybe a new aide at the home? Or was she dreaming of their mother and signals were crossed in her brain?

"I think of her sometimes too."

"I miss her."

Samantha placed a hand on Jordan's knee. "I miss her too."

"I need to fly to New York," Blake told Samantha nearly a week later.

"I was wondering when you'd start traveling again."

She knew Blake spent more time in his jet than in any of his homes. To have had him in her bed every night for nearly a month was a luxury she didn't think would continue forever.

"You can come with me."

They were drinking coffee on the veranda overlooking the ocean. A routine they'd both enjoyed since their return from Europe. Part of her wanted to jump at the invitation. But the practical part of her kept her from accepting. The internal clock in her head, counting backward with the time she had remaining as Blake's wife, was getting louder every day. The harder she tried to ignore the click, the worse it dug into her soul. There were times, like now, when he was smiling at her and encouraging her to travel with him, that Samantha felt like their marriage was more than a piece of paper—more than a mercenary act they'd both wanted. The way Blake made love to her or held her, even if they were both too tired to do anything else, dripped into her heart daily.

"I shouldn't," she sighed.

"Why not?"

"I've neglected Jordan. She didn't eat well while we were away, and she's been having trouble sleeping."

Blake reached for her hand. "You don't have to feel guilty for having a life, Samantha."

"I know. But it's hard. I'm all she has."

"You can always move her in here. We can hire full-time help."

It was the second time Blake had offered to relocate her sister. And if her marriage to Blake wasn't temporary, she'd take him up on his offer in a millisecond. "We've been over this. It wouldn't be fair to bring Jordan here, then pull her away after . . . She won't understand. That kind of stress results in illness and medical setbacks."

"But—"

"Please don't. I know you mean well, but I have to look out for her long-term interests."

Blake drank his coffee and dropped the subject. "I'm only going to be in New York for the weekend. Senator Longhill is having a small campaign dinner, and I should attend."

"He's the one who wants to give tax cuts to exports, right?"

"You have been listening."

Samantha tossed her unruly hair back and raised an eyebrow. "All this beauty and a brain—shocking, isn't it?"

"It's nice to have a conversation with a woman outside of the bedroom."

"Oh, ouch."

"I suppose that isn't fair."

"I hope not. Otherwise, I might have to draw a line between your words and what I've pictured as your father's personality."

Blake slammed his hand into his chest. "Oh, that hurt!"

"Honesty is our code word, my darling duke. I'm sure all the women haven't been that bad."

"*All the women*—you make it sound like I had a harem."

"You had a lot more than me."

He laughed. "That wouldn't have taken much, my darling duchess."

"Still . . ."

"I might have been able to talk to the previous women in my life, but I didn't confide in them like I do you." Blake's eyes narrowed, as if he were surprised to hear his own confession.

That proved something, didn't it? Blake had to

feel more for her than any of the temporary women in his life.

"So you need to schmooze the senator. Keep him on your side of the shipping fence."

"Exactly."

"When are you leaving?"

"Friday morning."

She pushed aside her cold coffee and squeezed Blake's hand. "I'll miss you."

His gaze traveled to hers before he pulled her hand to his lips for a tender kiss.

But her words weren't repeated back.

Blake used to look forward to cocktail parties. They were often a breeding ground for a one-night stand, or even longer affairs. As he walked around the room, overflowing with beautiful women, his thoughts were of his wife. Of Samantha being by his side, where they could mingle, drink, and comment about the different personalities in the room.

Her guilt over her sister was palpable. After returning from Moonlight their first day back, Samantha was close to tears. Jordan meant everything to her, and Blake was helpless to relieve any of the stress related to Jordan's care.

Sure, Jordan wouldn't understand when it came time for Samantha and her to move away, but surely the year would be worth it. With some effort, he and Sam had taken Jordan off

Moonlight's property for a trip to the zoo. The day had brought so many smiles to the girls' faces that Blake wanted to play hero and make it possible for them to be together more often.

The constant trips back and forth to Moonlight seemed to tire Samantha. She even skipped her morning exercise routine more than not. Blake didn't mind since it meant he could spend more time with her before going to work.

"Penny for your thoughts?" A familiar and unwanted voice sucked him out of his daydream. He straightened his shoulders, ready to face a woman scorned. "Vanessa."

Much taller than Samantha, Vanessa in heels nearly looked him in the eye. As always, she was perfectly manicured, from the top of her blonde head to the tips of her toes peeking through the jeweled stilettos cradling her feet.

The sweet smile she wore used to work, but now? He only heard the term Samantha had used for his ex. *Viper.*

"So nice of you to remember my name."

He supposed he deserved that. It wasn't as if he had the opportunity to break it off with her before he decided to pick a bride from Samantha's service.

"Don't be ridiculous." He kept his voice low and forced a smile on his face.

"I knew you were ruthless. I just never thought you were a coward. You could have told me about your plans. I might have been able to help you out instead of that mousy woman you're—"

Blake lifted the hand he held his drink in, cutting her off. "Have some respect, Vanessa. Samantha is my wife."

"For how long, Blake?" she whispered, leaning in.

His gaze narrowed, but his smile never fell. "Green isn't a good color on you."

Vanessa's lips fell into a tight line. "Jealous? Of her?" Her snide laugh brought a few eyes from the crowd toward them. "You've tied yourself to a woman raised by thieves. Trusting her with your last name will be your downfall."

"Thank you for your concern." The calmer he was, the more upset Vanessa became. How had he not seen this side of her when they'd been together?

"Women like her won't be happy until they own your soul. You'll wish it was me you'd asked to be your wife." The Viper said her piece and stood back.

He leaned in so only she could hear his retort. "The only thing I wish for, Vanessa, is that I'd met Samantha before meeting you." It was ugly, but he'd had enough of Vanessa's venom spewing about his wife.

Instead of splashing a glass full of liquor in his face, Vanessa did something unexpected. A sick smile spread over her lips, as if she held the world in her hands. "Oh my. You do care for the girl. Even better. Enjoy the pain, Blake." Then she walked away.

Blake extended his trip to New York through Wednesday, which would have sucked even more had Samantha been feeling better. She made good use of the time by making an appointment with her longtime doctor and friend to obtain a more convenient source of birth control.

Sitting on an exam table, wearing a flimsy hospital gown, Samantha braced her arms against the chill in the room. The stress of her marriage and worries about her sister kept her awake at night, and was wreaking havoc with her appetite.

A slight knock on the door proceeded Dr. Luna's entrance. In her midforties, Dr. Luna had been Samantha's doctor since her teenage years. She'd prescribed every antibiotic she'd ever taken and held her hand through the death of her mother.

"There you are. We were wondering when we were going to see you in here."

"Hi, Debbie." The formalities disappeared a long time ago, making it even easier to walk into the office.

Debbie hugged her before taking a seat on a rolling stool. "It's good to see you."

"Life got a little crazy."

"I know. It's not every day I see my patients' faces in the tabloids. I can't believe you're married. I didn't even think you were dating anyone."

"Blake and I didn't wait once we knew what we wanted." Which wasn't a complete lie, but certainly not the truth. So far, the line had worked on everyone Samantha had delivered it to. "Part of the reason I'm here is to get on those birth control pills we talked about."

Debbie smiled. "Of course. You'll wonder why you waited to take them once you start."

They talked about the pros and cons of the pill for some time before Debbie asked, "So what else is bothering you?"

"I'm not sure. I haven't had my usual energy lately. At first, I thought I was just being lazy, on an extended honeymoon. But my appetite is gone most of the day, and I'm more tired than normal."

Debbie scribbled a few notes on her chart. "Any fever?"

"No."

"Cough?"

"No."

"Nausea, vomiting, change in bowel habits?"

"A little queasy. But I think it's just because I go so long between meals."

"Hmmm." Debbie stood and removed her stethoscope from around her neck. After listening to her lungs, she said, "Lie back."

Samantha relaxed on the exam table while Debbie pressed on her belly. "Any pain?"

"No."

"When was your last period?"

Samantha glanced at the ceiling. "I'm due any day."

"When was your *last* one?"

"I don't remember. I've always been irregular." A sick feeling started to grow deep in her stomach.

Debbie tilted her head to the side. "What have you and Blake been using for birth control?"

"I'm not pregnant."

"I didn't say you were."

Samantha sat up, unable to lie still any longer. "Condoms. And we've never forgotten. We've blown through nearly every box he owned." A nervous laugh left her lips.

"Condoms have a two percent failure rate."

"Debbie, I'm not pregnant."

The doctor patted her on her arm before reaching behind her and grabbing a cup. "You know where the bathroom is. Let's remove pregnancy from possible reasons for your malaise so we can start looking for another source."

Samantha hopped from the table, ignoring the slight tremor in her hand. "Fine."

The next ten minutes were the longest in her life. Sam searched back in her calendar on her smartphone to the time before she and Blake had met, desperately trying to prove Debbie wrong before she walked back in the room.

But when the door opened and Debbie stepped

into the room, Samantha's heart plunged to the ground.

"Congratulations."

Sam jumped to her feet, shaking her head. "No."

"We can run a serum test, but these things are accurate. You're pregnant, not sick."

Everything stood still. The institutional-style clock on the wall ticked away the seconds, and the room closed in around her. Sam's chest started a rapid rise and fall as she struggled to take a deep breath. Tears stung the back of her eyes. "But we were careful."

Debbie patted her hand and encouraged her to sit back down. "I can see this is unexpected. Maybe you both wanted to wait to start a family, but it is what it is."

What was she going to do? Blake trusted her. How could this be happening? They'd been careful.

"Sit down." Debbie helped her onto the exam table again. "Take a deep breath. Everything is going to be OK."

"You don't understand." How could she? Debbie saw a newly married woman. Anyone else would be thrilled with the news of a baby.

"Then help me understand. What are you afraid of?"

The loving smile on Blake's face turning to hatred when he learns of the pregnancy. All the trust and mutual respect would end the minute she told him the news.

"It's not what we wanted," Samantha whispered, lost in her thoughts.

"You're not the first newlywed to get pregnant. I'm sure your husband loves you. He'll understand."

But he didn't love her.

A tear dropped down her cheek.

"Samantha?"

Her gaze traveled to her old friend, whose concern was etched into her face. "What's wrong? You didn't cry when your mother died or when your sister ended up in the emergency room." By now, Debbie was sitting beside her, her hands holding Samantha's.

Sucking in her bottom lip and forcing her eyes to dry, Sam shook her head. "Women are emotional creatures. Especially pregnant women." *Oh God, I'm pregnant.*

"Are you sure that's all it is?"

Unable to tell Debbie the truth, Samantha nodded. "I'm in shock. I need time to adjust."

"You've always adjusted, no matter what's thrown at you."

"I know."

"All right. Let's go over a few things you need to know. I'll be sending you to Dr. Marzikian . . ." Debbie outlined the first few months of pregnancy while Samantha listened with half an ear.

As she walked out of the office with a prescription for prenatal vitamins instead of birth control, Samantha never felt so alone in her life.

By the time she reached her car, the tears streamed down her face, and she was helpless to stop them.

Jeff Melina, Blake's personal lawyer, sat across from him, shaking a paper in the air. "Your father was a jackass."

"Tell me something I don't know."

"I've never seen a more ironclad will in my life. You'd think there'd be some loophole somewhere to negate what he's asking you to do."

Not the words Blake wanted to hear. "There has to be something."

Jeff tossed the papers on the desk. "I've looked. It's like your dad knew you'd marry long enough to collect, then divorce."

Confiding in his lawyer couldn't be avoided from the beginning. "Blows my plan all to hell."

"If you could find an unscrupulous doctor to jack up Samantha's medical records, saying she's unable to get pregnant . . . Oh, forget I said that."

Blake shook his head. "Samantha is seeing her doctor back in LA this week to get on the pill."

Jeff tapped his desk. "So you *are* sleeping with her. I didn't think you'd hold out."

"It was easier to give in than pretend we weren't interested." Blake could hardly wait for his flight later that night. He wanted to get home and sleep with her again. He missed her. When they'd spoken on the phone earlier in the day, she hadn't sounded right. Something was bothering her. He'd asked, but she'd let on like nothing was wrong.

"You know, there is something you haven't considered."

Blake thought himself a very thorough man. "What would that be?"

Jeff leveled his gaze to Blake. "Get her pregnant."

"What part about 'going on the pill' did you not understand?"

"You need two forms of birth control that first month."

Blake stood and started to pace. "Jesus, Jeff. You're kidding me, right?"

"Women have tricked men into unwanted pregnancies for centuries. They always want equal rights."

Blake shook him off. "Stop. I know you think I'm an ass, but I'm not that far gone." Obviously, his lawyer was, which might be a good thing in a courtroom, but not in this situation.

"It's my job to find a way to legally get you what you want. It's just a suggestion. You might try asking her."

"Ask her to get pregnant?"

"Why not? She obviously had a price the first time."

Blake's jaw started to ache. Jeff was treading a thin line, even if it held some truth. "She's not a hooker, Jeff."

"You're paying her ten million dollars to be your wife for a year, and you're sleeping with her."

Blake was over the desk in a heartbeat. Gripping the edge, he shoved his face next to Jeff's. "Don't go there."

"Whoa, boy, back off. I didn't realize you actually cared about her. I'm sorry." Jeff's face had gone ashen.

As Blake stepped away, he wondered if he'd have to find a new lawyer. Something in the way Jeff spoke about Samantha, as if she were no more than a piece of furniture, made him see red.

"I think we're done here." Blake needed to get out of the office before he started throwing punches.

Jeff smoothed his tie as he stood. "If she cares about you half as much as you seem to care for her, she might say yes to having your baby. Women are emotional that way."

Where had Blake heard that before?

Maybe.

Chapter Eleven

B lake was going to talk to Samantha tonight. Because keeping his father's shitty will to himself wasn't something he could do any longer. *Honesty* was their code word. Samantha's absolute trust in him would make him a better man. It scared him that Jeff thought he could force Samantha into a pregnancy or that Blake would use her that way. Had he earned that rotten reputation? Maybe he had. There weren't a lot of people who thought better of him, except maybe her.

Keeping her trust suddenly became paramount.

It was just past six when he walked into his Malibu home. The sound of Mary in the kitchen drew him there first.

"I hope you've made enough for two," he said, catching the woman's attention.

"Oh, you're home. Thank goodness. I thought I'd have to call you."

"Call me? Why? Is everything OK?" Blake glanced around the kitchen, expecting Samantha to walk into the room. She wasn't as used to Mary's services and often stood by to lend a hand with the chores.

"It's Samantha. She's hardly come out of your room all day."

Alarm bells went off in his head. "Is she sick?" He was already walking toward the stairs.

Mary followed behind him, dish towel in hand. "I don't know. She said she's fine. But she isn't eating, and I hear her crying."

Blake took the stairs two at a time and flew into his room. The door opened immediately, and he heard Samantha in the bathroom. Her sobs thrust a knife in his chest. When she swore, he thought it best to avoid an audience.

"I've got this," he told Mary.

Closing the door behind him, Blake stepped into the doorway of the bathroom and found Samantha sitting with her back to the tub, her head buried on her knees.

"Samantha?" He reached her side as he called her name.

When she brought up her tear-soaked eyes to meet his, something inside him ripped apart. What could possibly be so awful? For all the talk about women being emotional creatures, he hadn't seen it with the woman in front of him until now. Her lip quivered and a new round of tears started to fall.

"Honey, what's wrong?" He started pulling her into his arms, but she resisted his touch.

"They d-didn't work," she said.

"What didn't work?" He settled on his knees and kept his hands on her shoulders so she couldn't turn away.

Samantha reached for a box at her feet and waved it in front of his eyes. "These."

It took a few seconds to recognize what she held in her hand. Packages of condoms had been tossed around the bathroom as if Samantha had had a fight with the latex. Several boxes were on the counter, others by the tub.

"I don't understand what you mean."

Samantha picked up another box and threw it across the room at a wastebasket. "They didn't work!" she cried. She grabbed another packet, threw it, and missed.

Didn't work? What is she saying?

She buried her head on her knees again. "I'm pregnant."

Oh hell. Every nerve in his body jolted. Blake braced himself—for what, he didn't know. The feeling of dread didn't come. Dismay? No, that wasn't there, either. Shock? Yes, he was definitely shocked. The last thing he thought he'd come home to after an appointment with his lawyer discussing a need for an heir was to hear his temporary wife declare she was going to have his child. His astounded disbelief at knowing the trembling woman sitting on the floor of his bathroom was carrying his baby wouldn't set in for some time.

Damn, no wonder Samantha was so upset.

Blake gathered her in his arms.

She all but crawled into his lap.

"It's OK," he cooed in her ear.

Her sobs were so loud, so heartbreaking, that he felt a heavy guilt only the man who had put her in this position could feel. "It's going to be OK."

And it would be.

Someway.

Somehow.

"Shhh."

"I didn't m-mean for this to h-happen." She hiccupped between words.

"I know." He did know. Without any doubt, he knew Samantha wouldn't have ever planned this event.

Vanessa? Absolutely! If for no other reason than to be a duchess.

Jacqueline? Probably not. But then, she wasn't mother material.

Samantha? Hell no. His wife was too real for games and too real for this kind of deceit. At least with him. *Honesty* was their key word, after all.

Blake shifted on the balls of his feet and picked Samantha up to take her away from her war with the condoms. Lord, how was it he had so many boxes of the damn things, anyway? Oh yeah, Vanessa had sworn she was allergic to anything other than the brand he now saw littered all over the bathroom floor.

In their bedroom, he kept Samantha in his lap and crawled onto the soft surface of the bed. Samantha's upsetting sobs reduced to whimpers, and he felt her relax against his chest, finally succumbing to much-needed slumber. The entire time Blake held her, he stroked her hair, told her that he was there, and everything would work out.

He'd make everything work.

During the night, Samantha woke a few times, always with the weight of Blake's arm circling her waist or his fingers stroking her skin. Her exhausted sleep gave way to a blurry-eyed morning, with a headache that topped the charts. Add to that her typical lack of appetite and utter embarrassment over Blake catching her weeping in the middle of a bathroom floor surrounded by boxes of useless condoms, and Samantha didn't think things could get worse.

But then she remembered the pregnancy.

Point one for worse.

Her bladder forced her from Blake's arms and the warm bed. He didn't stir when she slid out and padded into the bathroom.

Sometime in the night, Blake must have cleaned up the mess she'd made. The boxes were gone or tucked away. Good, she mused. She didn't want to see another prophylactic for as long as she lived.

In the mirror, she noted the dark circles under her eyes, the smudges of makeup on her face. Her hair stuck out in a few places, and she hadn't managed to put on any nightclothes before collapsing into bed.

What a mess.

Forcing herself away from her reflection, Samantha took her time with a hot shower. As her thoughts shifted to what would happen next between her and Blake, she forced them away.

No more assuming. She'd work through every turn of their relationship with him and do her best to keep her emotions on a tight leash. This pregnancy wasn't something either of them had wanted. But it was. Sam knew she couldn't give away a child, or worse, terminate her pregnancy. She was a responsible adult, not a teenage kid without options.

The headache receded to the back of her head as she left the shower. A little cream on her face, some gel under her eyes, and she felt nearly human. When she exited the bathroom in a fluffy bathrobe, she expected to find Blake still asleep.

He wasn't.

Still in the rumpled clothing he'd slept in, he stood over a small tray he'd brought up from the kitchen. Samantha noticed coffee, milk, and juice, along with a couple of plates. On the serving plates were simple saltine crackers, toast, and hard-boiled eggs.

"What's this?"

Blake caught her elbow and encouraged her to sit. A serene smile met the corners of his mouth as he took the chair opposite her. "Pregnant women in their first trimester usually start their day off with bland food in order to settle their stomachs." He reported the facts that Samantha had already learned the hard way as if he were reading from a textbook.

"And where did you learn this?"

"Last night, when you slept, I used my phone for something other than looking up the latest market numbers. I brought coffee—decaf—but the articles I read said you probably wouldn't want it." He pushed the one glass of milk on the tray toward her. "But milk is a must for you and the baby."

With the word *baby,* Samantha felt tears sting her eyes again. So far, she'd only really looked at what was happening as a *pregnancy,* an event that changed everything. "This is so sweet."

"That's me, Mr. Sweet."

"Blake—" she started.

"Wait." He grasped her hand and bent down beside her. "We have a lot to talk about, but right now, let's hold off. You need to eat, and I could really use a shower." His thumb stroked the inside of her wrist as he spoke.

"But—"

He placed a finger over her lips. "Shhh . . ."

Samantha nodded, conceding to hold off their impending conversation.

Blake smiled and stood. But before he left the room, he placed his lips to hers for a tender kiss.

Maybe everything would work out.

An hour later, they both sat on the chaise lounges

on the back veranda overlooking the ocean. Blake wore tan shorts and a simple cotton shirt that stretched over his taut chest. The marine layer was far off the coast, giving the sun the opportunity to shine and the temperature to reach the high seventies.

Admittedly, Blake's idea of breakfast had worked wonders, except for the coffee; Samantha switched it for an herbal tea she now sipped from a warm mug.

Since leaving their bedroom, neither had said one word about the baby. But now the silence stretched between them as vast as the ocean.

"So?" Samantha heard Blake say.

"So." A nervous smile played on her lips. Her hands twisted in her lap. "I didn't mean for this to happen." It was the one thing she really needed Blake to understand. The whole reason he'd gone to her to find him a temporary bride was to eliminate a woman wiggling into his life permanently. And here she'd gone and done exactly that. Even if they ended their marriage after a year, a child would be there forever. Permanent.

"You've already said that."

"I need you to believe me."

"Look at me, Samantha."

She hesitated before bringing her eyes to his. There, she found a soft gaze and an easy smile. The same one he'd worn when she'd exited the shower. "I never thought for a minute you'd planned, wanted, or expected to be carrying my child."

A deep-suffering sigh escaped her lips. She spread her fingers over her thighs and forced some of the tension away. "Good. That's good."

Glancing back at the ocean, Blake said, "Did you suspect you were pregnant for long?"

Samantha shook her head. "No. I had no idea." She told him about her doctor visit, about how she'd learned of the pregnancy.

"And the doctor said condoms fail two percent of the time?"

"Yeah. I assumed that statistic was for complacent teens, not intelligent adults."

They mused over that for a few minutes. This time the silence was a comfort and not a rock in the road.

When Samantha glanced back over at Blake, his face had twisted into a painful expression. "What are you thinking?"

He shook his head. "I'm trying to find a way to ask you something."

"Just ask."

"But what if you give me an answer I don't want to hear?"

Wow, his honesty humbled her. For a brief moment, Blake appeared to her a man vulnerable to hurt and pain just like anyone else. Instead of that thought making him a lesser person, it made him all the more loveable.

She swallowed with the thought of love swimming in her head. Where had that come from? Damn, this pregnancy thing was already seeping into her emotions and making her a little crazy.

"If you want an answer, you'll have to risk the question. One thing you can count on with me is honesty."

The gray of his eyes met hers. "Do you want to keep the baby?"

Her heart kicked in her chest. "Do you want me to give it up—an abortion?" Her insides started to coil in on themselves. She couldn't read Blake's expression and didn't know what he was thinking. Was he just asking to find out where her mind was, or did he want to remove the pregnancy and go on as they were?

"I'll answer your questions after you answer mine."

That was fair. "I never considered anything other than having the baby."

Blake's shoulders slumped in. Was that relief or resolve? "Blake?"

He smiled. "I'm happy to hear that."

"Are you?"

"I am. I know this is all happening fast. It isn't anything like either of us thought it would be, but . . ."

"But?"

Blake pushed himself off the chaise and started

to pace. "This is the way I see it. We're not kids. Ten years ago, my thoughts would have been different—yours too, I think." He waited for her nod to continue. "When two people, who are not kids, find themselves pregnant, they go ahead and have the baby. The bonus here is that we're already married."

Oh my God. He's jumping really far ahead. "We didn't plan on staying married."

He stopped pacing and moved to sit on the edge of her chair. "I know. And maybe we won't. I think a baby changes things. No. I *know* a baby changes things. But until we both know exactly what we want, I say we move forward slowly."

"How does that look?"

"I like where we're at, Samantha. I like coming home to you, having you here. Until one of us wants to change that, I say we just continue on like we've been doing." His gaze searched hers.

"And after the year is up? After the baby is born?"

"The year doesn't have to change."

She knew that, but hearing him say it aloud tossed cold water on her face.

"You didn't want to hear that," he said, seeing her reaction.

"No. It's what we agreed on."

His hand slid up her calf and rested on her knee. "Do you want more than a year?"

"Right now, I don't know what I want. I just

found out I'm pregnant. I'm going to be a mother forever. That's the only solid thing I know is going to happen. Everything else is a big fat question mark."

"Let me give you one more solid thing, then." He patted her knee. "I'm going to be this child's father. I won't abandon you or our baby. You have my word."

She knew that. Deadbeat duke daddy didn't sound like Blake.

"Can I ask you something?" She knew she was about to open him wide with her question, but she needed to know his thoughts.

"Of course."

"Do you want more than a year?"

He paused, took a breath. "I think we owe it to our child to give each other the option for more time."

"Stay married for the baby?" Didn't that sound like a bad soap opera?

He didn't answer. Instead, he asked, "Do you like it here with me?"

What a silly question. Of course she did. "It doesn't suck."

He laughed. "So we push aside deadlines and contracts unless it does suck."

"Can we do that?"

"Honey, we can do whatever the hell we want."

She laughed then. A real laugh that hadn't come since she'd learned of the pregnancy. "Until it sucks, then. I think morning sickness sucks."

He laughed now, inching closer to her. "That doesn't count. I'm told delivery sucks too."

"Yeah well, that won't count, either. I'll get fat. That sucks."

Blake's hand inched up her thigh, past her hip, and lay on her now-flat tummy. "I'll bet you'll be adorable with a baby bump."

"Ha, you say that now. You'll think it sucks later, I'm sure."

His warm hand slid around her waist and up her rib cage. When it reached the underside of her breast, he brushed a thumb over her clothed nipple. "These will swell. That won't suck." His voice grew husky.

Samantha caught her lip between her teeth. "I'm told they'll hurt, and you won't be able to touch them. That will suck."

He leaned forward. The heat of his breath filtered over her lips. "I can handle all those sucky things if you can."

"Is that a challenge?"

His eyes sparkled with mischief. "Maybe."

"It sucks that you know how to push my buttons."

His lips lingered over hers, not touching, but so close. "I suck already?"

"I can handle it."

A brief brushing of his lips over hers wasn't enough. She leaned forward, wanting more. But he pulled back a tiny bit. "I'm glad it's you having my baby," he confessed. "You're going to be a wonderful mother."

"You don't know that."

"Yes, I do." He kissed her, really kissed her to the point where stars sparkled in her head and she forgot she was outside where the world could watch.

In Blake's arms, as he nibbled and kissed his way around her lips, neck, and jaw, the world didn't suck.

Chapter Twelve

The morning sickness got worse instead of better. And that sucked! Each day, Blake, trouper that he was, agreed that her morning "queasies" sucked, but he was going to help her through it until it got better. They agreed to keep a lid on the pregnancy through the first trimester, mainly because of the risk of complications and miscarriages. The doctor had assured them both after the second month they had nothing to worry about, but they waited to tell anyone anyway.

Samantha didn't even reveal anything to Eliza, which wasn't easy. But she thought it was best to keep her friend in the dark to avoid any slips in conversation.

True to his word, Blake stood beside her. There were times he needed to fly to Europe, but the trips were short, three days at most. It sucked when he was gone, but it was always wonderful when he came home.

The days started to drift together. The nights were always a memorable experience in Blake's arms. Then, just as the doctor had predicted, the morning sickness fairy stopped her daily visits.

Blake returned home after a day in the office, during which Samantha had spent her time removing furniture and wall hangings from a room across the hall from theirs. She was hoisting a small table from beside the bed when Blake's alarmed voice yelled from the door, "What the hell are you doing?"

She dropped the bedside table, nearly hitting her toe. "You scared me," she told him.

Blake stepped beside her, hands on his hips. "You shouldn't be lifting furniture." His eyes swept the room. "Have you cleared everything in here?"

All that remained was the big dresser, the bed, and tables. "Yeah, so? We talked about this being the baby's room," she whispered, careful not to let her voice carry to Louise, who was in their room cleaning.

"This is not OK," he said under his breath. "Louise, Mary?" he hollered.

"What are you doing?"

Louise made it to the room at a run, her eyes wide in alarm. "Is everything OK?"

"Go get Neil," Blake demanded.

Samantha grasped Blake's arm, her confusion muffled with alarm. No matter how much she nagged him to tell her what was wrong, he waited until Louise, Mary, and Neil stood before the two of them before he opened his mouth.

When he did, Samantha was shocked silent.

"Samantha's pregnant."

Her jaw dropped. They weren't going to say a thing to anyone until her next appointment with the doctor. Within seconds, she understood his motivations.

"I knew it," Louise said, glancing at Mary.

Mary shrugged her shoulders and offered a motherly smile. "Of course she is."

"You knew?" Samantha asked.

"Dear, we live here. Of course we knew."

Blake's face shifted to Neil.

"Don't look at me. I was in the dark."

"If you ladies knew Samantha was pregnant, then why would you allow her to move all this furniture up here?"

Neil's gaze darted around the room.

"She didn't want our help."

"I didn't need their help." Samantha defended herself, and them. "What's the big deal?"

Neil stepped forward. "Pregnant women shouldn't lift heavy stuff."

Blake smiled and patted Neil's back. "Someone who understands."

"Is that what this is about? You don't think I'm capable of clearing out this room?" Oh, now she was just getting pissed. Of all the sexist things . . .

"From now on, I don't want Samantha lifting anything other than a dinner plate or shopping bag. And if the shopping bag is heavy, not even that." Blake wasn't talking to her, but over her to the staff.

"Now, you wait just a minute—"

Mary backed up and motioned to Louise. "I think we need to leave."

"Blake is right." Neil voiced his opinion. "Let me help with this stuff. No need for you to hurt yourself or the baby."

Samantha shot out an arm when Neil moved around them to pick up the table she'd been struggling with. "Hold on. I'm pregnant, not an invalid. The doctor didn't say anything about restrictions."

"Neil," Mary barked, "I think we should leave Samantha and Blake to work this out without our help."

The three of them quietly slipped away, leaving Samantha holding her tongue, tightly controlling her anger, while Blake squared his jaw with determination.

"I thought we agreed to hold off telling anyone about the baby."

He glanced around the room. "I think we missed the mark on that one. Damn, Samantha, you could have gotten hurt up here moving this stuff around."

"It's just stuff."

"Heavy stuff that you shouldn't be lifting."

"Oh please—"

Blake lifted his hand, silencing her protest. "What if you had lifted this table"—Blake kicked the wood at his feet—"and started to have stomach pains?"

A shiver of worry caught her unaware. "That probably wouldn't happen."

"But what if it did?"

Samantha shifted her eyes around the room, noticing the size of the queen bed for the first time, the bulky weight of the dresser she was determined to scoot out of the room before Blake had interrupted her.

Maybe Blake had a point. "I can lift shopping bags," she said under her breath.

Blake stepped into her personal space and pulled her into his arms. His hands felt cold as they rubbed up and down her back, and she could hear the rapid thump of his heart in his chest. He'd been worried, really taken back by her actions. The emotional woman in her sighed with contentment that he cared. The independent woman in her shook a tiny fist in the air.

"Please promise me you'll ask for help in the future."

Promises weren't something she offered unless she could deliver, so she didn't rush the words he wanted to hear from her lips.

Blake eased back and took her head in his hands. "Promise me."

"I was feeling so good today. I think the morning sickness is behind me."

"Promise me." Blake didn't let up his plea.

"OK, fine. I won't lift anything heavy. Satisfied?" Her clipped words came out a bit harsher than she'd wanted, but Blake didn't seem to mind. His smile reached his eyes.

"You promise?"

"I promise!" She pushed against his chest. "Jeez, do you always get your way?"

Nodding, Blake offered, "I promise to jump on anything you need lifted. You won't have to nag me to get stuff done."

"OK, buster, put your muscles where your mouth is. I want this room clear so I can prep the walls, paint."

Blake's eyes shot up, and a frown fell on his lips. "Paint fumes?" he questioned.

Already, she knew there would be more promises made before night fell.

In the end, she promised to leave the heavy work to Blake and anyone he hired to make it happen, and Samantha had rein to point, spend, and dictate as many changes as she deemed necessary.

Instead of announcing the coming heir to his father's lawyers with written correspondence, Blake opted for a much grander delivery. As soon as Samantha felt well enough to travel, they planned their trip to his ancestral home to tell the rest of the family.

The small dinner party rumbled with excitement until Blake finally hushed the family and took Samantha by the hand. "I think by now most of you have guessed why we asked you here tonight," he began.

"You know how much I adore assumptions," his mother called from the far end of the table.

Those around laughed and waited for his next words.

"Samantha and I are expecting a child in late January."

"I knew it." Gwen hopped to her feet and circled the table to hug Samantha and then him.

Congratulations and a chorus of well-wishes rose. If anyone in the room questioned when Samantha had become pregnant, none said a word.

Howard caught his eyes from the far end of the table, and his lips fell into a straight line. Blake blamed his father for the strain on his relationship with his cousin. If the man hadn't named him as the second in the will, perhaps Blake and Howard could have been closer. Sadly, that wasn't the case. Paul leaned forward and whispered something to his son, and Blake turned his attention back to his wife.

Samantha radiated pride and a special glow that many people spoke of when they talked of pregnant women. She wore a summer dress with short sleeves and belt around her still-small waist. He noticed a swell in her breasts, which responded with more sensitivity when they made love. Each day he woke to a new wonder. At the last doctor's appointment prior to this trip over the pond, they'd heard the tiny fluttering beat of their child's heart. Tears had welled in Samantha's eyes, and his throat had clenched in a painful grip. An instant attachment to the child not yet born felt more solid than anything had in his life. Well, nearly anything, he mused.

His gaze fell to his wife in the sea of people, pulling her in for a hug. Identifying his love for their child collided with another reality.

His love for Samantha.

Instead of scrambling away from potentially devastating emotions, Blake held them close to his chest like a good hand in a game of poker. He had plenty of time to decipher Samantha's feelings before he opened himself wide. It wasn't routine for Blake to play any cards until he knew he'd win the game.

Parker sequestered himself with Blake for a few moments before leaving the party at the end of the night. "I see you've secured all your father's requests."

Put like that, Blake felt a slimy film of dirt slide over his consciousness. Although he hadn't done anything deviant in obtaining his ultimate goal, the fact that he'd never told Samantha about the need for an heir weighed on him.

"So it seems," Blake said.

Parker held out his hand for Blake. "We'll meet again after the birth and sign papers. Congratulations again."

"Thank you."

As Blake watched Parker leave his home, he

felt the eyes of someone on him. When he turned, he found Samantha standing in the hall. "Your father's lawyer, right?"

Blake gave a curt nod. "They were close friends."

Samantha moved to his side and placed a hand around his waist before leaning into him. "I guess he has no need to doubt your intentions now."

Her gaze drifted toward the door.

"He will doubt until our baby's born, I'm afraid."

Samantha leaned her head on his shoulder and stifled a yawn behind her hand.

"You're tired," Blake announced. "We should get you to bed."

"But there are still a lot of people here on our behalf."

"People who will just have to do without us."

When Samantha didn't offer any more resistance, he knew the extent of her exhaustion and ushered her to bed.

Blake and Samantha stopped over in New York for a couple of days on their way back to California. While Blake met with his lawyer, Sam braved the sweltering heat of Manhattan and did a round of completely unnecessary shopping.

As much as she tried to focus on the need for maternity clothes, the baby section of the department stores sang to her in a way she hadn't expected. Maybe it was because everyone who needed to know she was pregnant already knew, but Sam had the strange urge to buy one of everything.

Not knowing the sex of the baby made some things more difficult, but a green baby outfit here and a yellow one there worked. She found a hand-knitted white blanket to wrap the baby in when they came home from the hospital. With several bags in hand, Samantha was shuffling through tiny socks and plush toys when she felt a tap on her shoulder.

Cooing over a musical rattle, she twisted to see who wanted her attention.

The Viper stood before her, all blonde and bombshell. "Why am I not surprised to find you here?" Vanessa all but hissed from between her pink lips.

Samantha really didn't care what the other woman thought, and certainly didn't want to become engaged in a conversation with her. What were the chances of accidently running into the woman in a city the size of New York, anyway? Sam knew she lived there, but what were the odds?

"Vanessa."

Vanessa tipped a finger at the elephant rattle Samantha held. "Isn't this cute? So when are you expecting your bundle of joy?"

"It's really none of your business." Samantha put the toy down and turned to walk away.

"Let me guess"—Vanessa blocked her exit, leaving Samantha between a bookcase full of baby paraphernalia and a venomous snake— "before Blake's birthday?"

Easy guess. Not that it mattered. "Are you so envious, Vanessa? So jaded that Blake didn't marry you?"

Vanessa tossed her head back with a laugh. "Oh please. That manipulating bastard? It's easier to see his true nature when you're not close to him. Too bad you didn't notice before." Vanessa let her voice drift off as her eyes settled to Samantha's stomach.

Sam placed a hand over her waist, as if protecting her child from the woman's stare.

"Blake is one of the most caring people I've known."

"Blake cares only for himself. I wonder, though, did he ask you to have his baby, or did he 'accidentally' forget to cover up one night?" Vanessa used her fingers in air quotes.

Their conversation was toppling off a mountain of weird and plunging toward bizarre. "I don't have time for you, Vanessa. If you'll excuse me."

Samantha edged away, but Vanessa grasped her arm.

"My God, you really have no idea, do you?"

Sam tugged her arm, but the other woman didn't let go. A strange wave of panic hit her.

Much like the feeling a dog must get before an earthquake happens, everything in Samantha went silent.

"You know Blake needs an heir for his inheritance, don't you?"

What?

Vanessa's smile lifted high on her face, and her hand drifted back to her side. "Poor girl. How did he do it, I wonder? Did he hide your pills? Or poke holes in the condoms?"

Sam's jaw started to ache. She held her control so tight she felt like the muscles in her neck were ready to snap. What the hell was Vanessa talking about?

Then Parker's words returned to remind her: *I see you've secured all your father's requests.* Not giving Vanessa anything more, Samantha turned on her heel and fled the store.

The furnace heat of New York plastered her hair to her head as she put distance between herself and the Viper.

Blake needs an heir for his inheritance. The words echoed inside her brain. Could they be true? If they were, it made sense why Blake had accepted the news so calmly. It had been the one thing Samantha thought he didn't want from his temporary marriage. No wonder he hadn't flipped a fuse when she'd announced her pregnancy. He hadn't so much as shrugged a shoulder. Had he even been surprised?

No, she didn't think so now that she thought about it.

It wasn't as if he needed to make more promises to her because of the baby. Not really.

He'd offered to be a good dad and be there for the baby anyway.

Refusing to let emotion completely cloud her mind, Samantha hailed a cab and worked her way uptown to the condominium Blake owned on the East Coast.

She'd visited there twice now, both on trips to and from Europe. It was just after noon when she made her way into the cool air of the secured building.

Keeping her sunglasses on, Samantha waved at the doorman and made it to the bank of elevators, avoiding any conversation.

Unlike their Malibu home, there weren't maids or cooks to contend with here.

Tossing the forgotten bags on the sofa, Samantha turned on the laptop in the extra room Blake used as an office. She needed to find out a few facts before confronting Blake about Vanessa's claims.

The birth rate of people using condoms had bugged her from the beginning. Responsible men like Blake used condoms their entire adult lives and managed to avoid the title of Daddy. So what had changed? Why with her?

As her fingers clicked away on the keyboard, she pulled up several health and wellness sites about condoms, their use, their effectiveness. It wasn't until she found a website titled "Why do condoms fail?" that she held any hope of finding anything useful.

The site was full of typical information, including breaking condoms. But that hadn't happened—not that Samantha had noticed, in any event. There were interviews with women who ended up in the two percent category. On several occasions, they confessed to improper use, breaks, expired latex.

Even then, she and Blake had had sex for only a month before she found herself pregnant. It was as if they hadn't used any protection at all.

How could a man ensure a woman's pregnancy?

Even in the heat of desire, they'd been responsible.

Samantha pushed away from the desk and worked her way into their bedroom. They'd used the room en route to their reception, so it stood to reason that the condom they used had been pulled from the box here in the bedside table.

The box was still there.

Samantha glanced at the expiration date, which was still several months out. The box was nearly empty. She took the box into the bathroom and pulled one of the foil packets out. Careful not to cause any damage, she opened the packet and removed the contents. It didn't look damaged.

On instinct, she pressed its edges to the faucet

on the sink and turned on the water. At first, nothing happened.

But as she turned off the water and watched the tip of the condom, a small drop started to leak from the tip.

Samantha's heart fell deep inside her chest as she watched a steady drip, drip, drip of leaking fluid exit the condom.

Her lip trembled, and her hands started to shake. The rubber dropped into the sink, and Samantha removed another one. The same thing happened.

Unable to believe her eyes, or what her mind was screaming, Samantha removed yet a third condom from the package and returned to the room. She turned off the overhead lights, placed the foiled packet over a single bulb from a lamp, and turned it on.

A single miniscule beam of light beamed through the foil like a beacon.

In all their honesty, all their talk of being open, Blake had executed his need for an heir and manipulated her into thinking it was no more than an accident.

Everything inside her screamed. How could she have been so naive? So gullible? Tears streamed down her face as she cleaned up the condoms, tucking them into the far side of the trash to go unnoticed.

She pocketed one condom in her purse and left two more in the box by the bedside.

There was nothing Samantha hated more than being used as a pawn for another person's needs.

How could the man she'd fallen in love with do this to her?

How was she going to survive without him?

"Samantha's pregnant," Blake told Jeff in the privacy of the lawyer's office.

"So the tabloids spoke the truth for once." Jeff waved a royalty rag under his nose and tossed it on the desk.

Blake hadn't seen the coverage, but only glanced at the telling title. "Duke to Daddy" topped the page.

"I just thought you should hear it from me instead of assuming anything. Things should go smoothly after my birthday next year."

"I'll ask Parker's man to send the necessary papers the week of your birthday, and we'll have everything hammered out within a few short weeks after." Jeff sat back and smiled. "I can't believe you did it."

"Did what?" Blake placed an ankle over his knee as they spoke.

"Talked her into getting pregnant. What did you offer—ten more million?"

Blake's skin crawled with Jeff's words. "It wasn't like that. Fate simply lent a hand."

"Really?"

"Accidental pregnancies happen all the time."

"So the women badgering my clients for child support say. In my experience, accidents are made."

Blake supposed he saw that comment coming. "You forget that I'm the one benefiting from this baby even more than Samantha. I'm positive she's done nothing unsavory."

Jeff leaned forward in his chair. "You're sure?"

"Positive."

Jeff's hand reached over the table. "My congratulations."

After shaking the man's hand, he went on to more pressing matters. "About the cameras in Samantha's home, did we find anything?"

Jeff opened a few papers on his desk and spread them out. "As you know, Vanessa confronted Samantha, but when we followed her, we didn't see her return or come in contact with any private investigator. Our own PI snapped a few pictures, but the men and women she's with here all pan out. They're either businessmen like yourself or professionals like me."

Blake noticed the familiar image of Vanessa, dark sunglasses and porcelain features, as she sipped coffee or spoke on her phone. One image caught in his mind as more than familiar. Vanessa speaking to a woman he'd seen before but couldn't quite place. "Do you know who this is?"

"A law student . . . Or was it a legal secretary?" Jeff asked himself. "Secretary, I believe."

Blake's mind shifted over the rest of the photos.

Only the one struck him as strange.

"We think the cleanup man with the cameras was paid to ditch them. He never led us anywhere but to a trash can. We can't find anything linking Parker or your cousin to the States. It's like a huge dead end, or dump, as they say."

Blake supposed it didn't matter at this point, but he still wanted to nail whoever had invaded Samantha's privacy.

"Keep working on it." Some might think a lawyer was used only for legal representation, but in his life, help begot help. And Jeff knew people who could keep a watchful eye on anyone and anything.

"I will."

Blake grasped the picture of Vanessa and the secretary. Until he could name the woman in the photo, he'd keep looking at it.

There was no greater impact than seeing a set of bags packed and on a doorstep to know a problem was erupting. Or at least Samantha hoped.

Blake had lied to her. Instead of coming to her with a problem they could have possibly found a solution for, he'd manipulated the situation to produce an outcome to suit his needs. Memories of her father's arrest, of the feelings Dan had provoked with his deceit, surfaced.

Blake knew her secrets, her insecurities, and had played on them to get what he needed.

Yes, together, they'd embarked on this deal with the devil. Marry to suit the needs of a dead man and both leave richer in the end. But that had changed as their attraction grew and a child had been conceived.

Samantha grasped her belly that had just started to stretch beyond the limits of her jeans. She held a glass of wine in her hand. She'd only sipped once. Stomaching more wasn't an option. For as much as she wanted to hurt Blake, she wanted nothing to do with harming her child.

Damn him. Damn him for making her love him, trust him, and then blowing that all to hell.

The key in the lock twisted, and Samantha set her gaze on the bags sitting by the door. She lifted the glass of wine in her hand. Perhaps she should have been an actress. Blake had certainly missed his calling.

Out of the corner of her eye, she noted Blake's hesitation two steps into the room. "Samantha?"

She'd thought of what to say all afternoon. The image of her running, not saying a thing to his face and leaving him with the knowledge that she'd simply left, held some merit. But in the end, she couldn't leave without a final word of disapproval.

"When were you going to tell me?" she said as he inched into the room, as if he were walking into a minefield full of bombs ready to explode.

"Tell you what?"

"You spent time at your lawyer's today. Surely you discussed the will."

Blake held still.

Samantha slowly turned her head in his direction, but she took a considerable amount of time before leveling her eyes to his. When she did, she noted how he glanced between the wineglass in her hand and to her face. Even now, she thought, he considered their child before her. For effect, she brought the beverage to her lips, pretended to drink, and then lowered the glass.

"What's going on, Samantha?" His gaze shot to the bags she'd packed so she could make a some-what graceful exit.

"I thought we were going to be honest with each other. What happened to that, Blake?"

"Sam, what are you talking about?"

Unable to sit, she stood and placed the wine on the table, nearly spilling it. To Blake, she probably looked as if she'd been drinking too much. *Just as well,* she thought. "Your father's will—what did it really say? Or did you think I'd never find out?"

Blake's eyes grew wide, and his lips fell into a tight line.

His expression said all she needed to know.

Guilt . . . maybe a little remorse. But for what? Remorse over being caught in a lie?

"I didn't think it was important."

"You didn't think telling me your father mandated an heir was important for me to know?"

Blake shut his eyes, accepting her words.

And that said everything.

Killing the tears before they had a chance to fall, Samantha squared her shoulders and stormed toward her duke. "Honesty was what defined us. But you couldn't trust me with that, could you?"

Blake opened his eyes and watched her approach. "I didn't want to burden you with details."

Her jaw dropped in a sarcastic laugh. "Burden me? God, you actually believe yourself. You're no better than your father. You tell everyone around you how it's going to be, force your will on others, and they fall into step."

He reached out, but Samantha sidestepped away from his hands. "Don't touch me. Those days are over."

"Samantha, please, I know this seems—"

"I know what this is, Blake. You lied to me about your father's will."

"I found out about the second condition after we were married."

Her stomach twisted. This stress couldn't be good for the baby. She forced a big breath of air into her lungs and blew it out slowly. "That may be, but it didn't stop you from making sure you'd win in the end, did it?"

Blake shook his head. "What are you saying?

231

We both knew the risks when we slept together."

"Don't you dare lie. Come clean, Blake. I've had men bigger than you shove deceit in my face for a lot longer. I might have let my emotions get the better of me for the last several months, but I'm not a complete pushover." She waited for the confession about how he'd reduced himself to poking holes in condoms to get what he wanted, expecting his plea for her forgiveness.

Instead, she received a blank look.

Without another word, Samantha walked over to her bags.

"What are you doing?"

"I'm leaving. Or did the bags confuse you?"

"Jesus, Samantha, we can work this out. I should have told you about the codicil."

"You *should* have told me. I would have given you everything, Blake." Her heart broke into a thousand pieces as the next words left her mouth. "All you had to do was ask."

Samantha turned around and walked out of Blake's life.

She half expected him to rush after her. But then, that was the romantic in her, the part of her that believed she meant something to him other than the broodmare she'd become. It didn't matter if she left. Blake would still have his heir.

And she'd have a lifetime of regrets.

Chapter Thirteen

S he walked out. Dammit, she left him with no more than one simple omission on his part.

Women are emotional creatures. Pregnant women, more than most. She needed time to blow off some steam. He understood that, but she'd come back.

Yet, as the minutes rolled into an hour and the one hour into two, Blake knew his omission weighed on his wife a lot more than he could imagine.

When his phone rang an hour later, he jumped to answer it.

"Samantha?"

"It's Jeff. Sorry, I can call back if you're expecting another call."

The last person he needed to speak with was his lawyer. Blake swirled the triple-malt scotch around in his glass before tilting the amber liquid back in his throat. "What is it?"

"Are you OK? You sound like shit."

"Thanks."

"OK, not in the mood for chitchat. Just thought you'd like to know that my PI saw Vanessa corner Samantha in a department store today. According to him, Vanessa seemed a little aggressive, and instead of leaving angry, Samantha left upset."

Vanessa?

"Did your guy hear the conversation?"

"No. He doesn't get that close. Is everything OK?"

Blake's mind ticked. So that's how Sam had found out about the will. Vanessa must have known about the will. But how?

Then the image of the woman in the picture swam in his eyes. "Fuck! The woman . . ."

"What?"

"In the picture with Vanessa. Leona. No. Neo . . . Naomi. Naomi something. Works as a fucking secretary for Parker and Parker." Blake slapped a hand to his forehead. "Vanessa knows Parker's legal secretary, Jeff."

"Your ex knows the right hand of your father's lawyer?"

"Which means Vanessa knew all along about my father's will." No wonder the woman was so willing to be a duchess.

"You think she was behind the cameras in Samantha's apartment?"

"I'd bet good money on it."

"So what did she say to your wife?"

"Enough to make her leave." No use sugar-coating the situation. It wasn't as if Jeff wouldn't be one of the first to know if there were legal trouble.

"Left? What do you mean?"

"Never mind. I'll get in touch in a few days. In

the meantime, draft a letter to Parker dictating that a breach in confidentiality might render anything from his office null and void."

Dammit. He was a tyrant. No better than his dead father. Even now, in the midst of losing his wife, his child, he thought about the eventual end.

"On second thought, do nothing. No, wait . . . I do need you to do something else."

Blake spelled out his wishes, leaving no doubt what he wanted to happen.

An hour later, Blake found himself in front of his computer. He'd opened his browser expecting to see if Samantha had used it to find a flight to California.

When the history pointed to websites about condoms and pregnancy rates associated with them, he took a step back.

If Vanessa knew about the will, she knew about the need for an heir . . . Vanessa would have manipulated a pregnancy with him if she'd been given enough time. Thankfully, Blake had met Sam and put an end to his relationship with Vanessa. All that was left of that woman were the boxes of condoms she'd left behind.

"Son of a bitch!"

Blake shoved out of the chair and rushed into the bedroom. The box of leftover condoms in the drawer only had two in the box. He lifted a package to his eye, didn't see a thing, and then held it to the light.

Heat slammed into his chest when he saw a pinprick hole through the middle. "Oh God. Samantha."

His wife must have found these and thought the worst of him. And why not? It wasn't as if he'd told her the condoms had come from an ex.

Dammit, what was she thinking? She probably thought he was worse than Dan, just another man in her life who'd let her down, one who'd lied to get what he wanted. He wanted to call her back, force her to listen to him. What proof did he really have?

The image of Vanessa shot into his mind, and his pissed meter struck an all-time high. The anger he harbored for his father was a walk in the park compared to his need for revenge on his ex-lover.

Blake picked up the phone and called in a few favors. Carter had several friends in the NYPD. "Carter, I need you to do something for me."

Twenty-four hours later, Blake stood in front of the exclusive high-rise condominium complex, twisting his hands so hard Samantha would be proud. Not going to her had been hell. But he wouldn't confront Sam until Vanessa paid for what she'd done.

The sickly sweet floral perfume that followed Vanessa wherever she went assaulted his senses before he saw her. His heartbeat sped, not because of any residual feelings or desires for the woman, but with a deep-seated hatred. If she ruined his chances of a future with his wife, he'd find a way to ruin her. He made the promise to himself as he pushed away from the building and caught Vanessa's arm.

She gasped, twisted toward him, and then relaxed when she recognized the face behind the hand. "Blake? Darling, how are you?"

Out of the corner of his eye, he saw Carter and an undercover detective walk into the high-rise, completely undetected by the woman in front of him.

"I wondered if you had a minute." His skin crawled just thinking of being agreeable to her for the time it took the officers to search her home.

Her guarded expression shifted, as if she were unsure of what Blake was going to do. Their last encounter had been less than pleasant, but he didn't want her running off.

"I didn't think we had anything more to say to each other."

"I wanted to thank you for your warning." He rolled the lie off his tongue so easily even he believed it.

"Warning? About what?"

"About Samantha not being happy until she owned my soul. I thought I could do a nice quiet marriage, nothing packed with too much emotion or loyalties . . ." He let his words trail to see what Vanessa would do with the baited hook.

"Oh, Blake." She removed her sunglasses and sent him a pointed stare. She pushed out her lower lip with an expression that mirrored sympathy. "What happened?"

"I'm not sure. This pregnancy, I wasn't expecting it. It isn't like we weren't careful." He glanced around them, pulled her away from prying eyes, and lowered his voice for effect. "How can a woman get pregnant using condoms? I doubt it isn't mine, but . . ."

Vanessa hung her head. "Oh my. I once heard of a woman tampering with the condoms to ensure a pregnancy. Do you think she'd do something that severe?"

Blake closed his eyes, thankful his sunglasses hid the majority of his expressions. Bile bubbled in the back of his throat. What a conniving, vengeful bitch. He sent a mental signal to whoever was watching for the men in Vanessa's apartment to hurry the hell up. Every second in this woman's presence was one Blake wasn't sharing with his wife.

"I can't imagine . . ." he said.

"I should be angry at you. After all, you up and married her shortly after we'd—"

Blake sighed. "I . . ." The phone in his pocket buzzed. He shifted it to his palm and read Carter's text: *Got her!*

The lie he'd been about to spew died on his tongue. Instead, he let the truth sing. "I love her."

"What?"

"Love. Trust. Things I never felt with you."

Vanessa, who had moved closer to him than he ever wanted her to be again, shifted back. The color in her face drained.

"You just said—" Blake removed his glasses, let the tightness in his jaw show as his eyes narrowed to daggers. From Vanessa's expression, she felt them drive deep into her core.

"We've named you Viper. Do you know that, Vanessa?"

"What?"

"Your venom has poisoned enough. Did you really think you'd get away with it? Right now, in your condo, the police have searched and found everything they need."

Vanessa started to edge back. Her stiletto heels caught, and she nearly fell. As she righted herself, her eyes burned with pure hatred. "I don't know what you're talking about."

"Oh, I think you do."

Blake noticed a black-and-white pull up along the sidewalk.

Vanessa's eyes shot to the police and back to him.

"I did nothing illegal."

She'd hired people to do her dirty work, like the man posing as a worker to plant cameras in Samantha's apartment. Taking illicit photos of him and his wife was against the law. He'd find

239

whatever legal means he could to make her pay. "We'll let the courts decide that." She might not spend years behind bars, but Blake wanted every man who crossed the Viper's path to know what kind of snake she was.

The first night back in California, Samantha had shifted a cot next to Jordan's bed in her room and did her best to sleep.

She'd screwed things up. She'd have the money to take care of her sister, but in the end, Samantha had a new responsibility. A child would come into this world, born of a selfish, domineering father and a mercenary mother. What a pathetic pair they were.

And all for what?

Samantha could have made things work, could have managed to take care of Jordan without Blake's millions. But the simple way was to take his offer and color her life easier.

Eliza had pushed her boyfriend out the door when she'd found him snooping through her files about the new female clients she'd rounded up for Alliance. That left room in Eliza's apartment for two brooding women who needed to spend their time discussing the merits, or lack thereof, of men.

Unlike other times, Samantha wasn't able to do anything more than eat, sleep, and stare out into the courtyard and watch people walk by.

The bone-deep pain inside her chest simply didn't let up. At one point, she considered calling her doctor, thinking something must be wrong, but then she realized a broken heart held physical pain to the degree she hadn't felt since her mother's death.

Three days after her arrival home, Eliza left Samantha alone to brood in peace.

When a knock sounded on the front door, she stared at it. She wasn't expecting anyone, so she continued to sit on the couch without moving. The knocking continued until she forced herself to her feet.

Although she'd expected Blake at some point, seeing him standing in a worn shirt, faded tan slacks, and a five o'clock shadow cut open a weeping wound.

"What are you doing here, Blake?"

"We need to talk."

The tears were all dried up, and she refused to give their child any more stress than it had already endured.

"I don't have anything more to say."

As she started to shut the door, Blake's foot stepped over the threshold, stopping it. "I love you."

Samantha's hand hovered in the air. She shut her eyes against the pain his words evoked. Another day, another time, she'd have thrown herself in his arms with his confession, but now they came too late.

Even if he did love her, it didn't change a thing. "Did you hear me?"

"Why are you doing this to me?" The pain in her chest started to swell. Her breath caught and threatened to choke the air clogging into her lungs.

"Five minutes, Samantha. Give me five minutes. Please."

Had she ever heard Blake beg for anything?

She opened the door wider and accepted his presence in the room.

He handed her a paper. "Look at page three."

"What is it?"

"Just look."

Samantha turned the pages to where he'd directed and noticed a picture of the Viper and another unidentified woman being escorted into a police station. "What is this?"

"Vanessa used her friend at my father's lawyer's office to obtain confidential files regarding the will."

Which explained why the woman had known about the will and Samantha was left in the dark.

"So?"

"I found the condoms, Samantha. All of them."

Samantha shook her head and lifted her uncertain eyes to Blake's. "All of them?"

"Vanessa wanted to trap me into marriage. She knew I needed an heir before I did. She concocted a story about a latex allergy and supplied me with condoms. I had no idea she'd altered every one of them. She went so far as to open the boxes and glue them back together."

Blake was standing closer now, his hands reaching out to take hers. As the shock of his words washed over her, Samantha stared absently at his chest.

"Vanessa poked holes in the condoms?"

"It wasn't me."

Her mind clogged with the new information. Samantha backed away, dislodging her hands from Blake's, and sat on the sofa. The picture of Vanessa surrounded by the police solidified Sam's belief that the woman was a snake.

"The police found files on Vanessa's computer—video files—of us."

The woman was sick. Blake was lucky to have escaped her clutches. But her actions didn't excuse his. "Why didn't you tell me about the will?"

Blake sat on the table facing her. When his hands came to rest on her knees, she jumped. A hurt expression flashed on Blake's face before he moved his hands away. "At first, I wanted to see if there was some way around it. When my lawyer exhausted his resources, I planned to tell you. When I arrived home, I found you in the bathroom declaring war on the condoms. One day bled into the next, and it just didn't seem important any longer."

"That's no excuse."

"I know that now. But it's the truth, Samantha. It wasn't until last week when I saw my father's lawyer that I thought I'd need to say something to you. The risk of losing you kept my lips sealed." Blake dared another touch; this time she didn't flinch. His pleading eyes sought hers. "I'm sorry. I should have done so many things differently. And if you'll give me another chance, I promise to never keep anything from you again."

Samantha's lip started to tremble, so she sucked it into her mouth to control it. Blake's explanation, his motivations, were understandable. But the truth was, their marriage was still one of convenience—destined to end in heartache. Now or later, but it had an end date on it. Living with that open-ended question wasn't something Samantha could do any longer. It wasn't fair to either of them—or the baby.

"Can you forgive me?"

Samantha closed her eyes, and when she opened them, she stared deep into Blake's. "I forgive you."

He started to smile, but Sam shook her head.

"Blake, wait. I can't do this. I thought I'd be able to play house, play wife, and be able to leave after the year was up, but I can't."

"But—"

"No, wait," she cut him off. "I know you didn't want emotional attachment, but I couldn't help falling in love with you any more than I could stop breathing and survive."

This time when Blake lifted his lips into a smile that reached all the way to the sparkling gray of his eyes, there was no holding it back. "You love me?" he whispered.

"Which is why we need to end things now," she explained.

Blake closed his eyes, shook his head, and let out a gasp. "What?"

"It's hard enough being pregnant. This pain in my heart, the not knowing if you're going to decide to make good on the end date of our marriage contract, isn't something I can live with." Even looking at him now caused her heart to skip. How could she go through the next eight months thinking he'd ask her to leave?

"Did you hear me say I love you?"

"Yes, but—"

Now he held up a finger to her lips and silenced her. "I love you, Samantha Harrison, and if you're waiting for the day I ask you to leave my life, you'd best be willing to wait a lifetime. I've already had Jeff draw up my will. The one that gives you and our baby everything if something were to happen to me."

"What?"

Instead of explaining himself, Blake bent down on one knee and lifted her hand to his lips for a tender kiss. "This might be ass-backward, but will you marry me? Not because of some contract, a will, or money, but because you love me and want to be my wife for now and forever?"

"What?" Her voice dropped a full octave, which for her was deep.

"You've made me a better man, Samantha. Say you'll marry me."

"Oh, Blake"—she knelt down beside him—"we're already married."

He smiled, caught her face in his hands. "Is that a yes?"

She loved him so much. Saying no wasn't an option. "Forever is a long time."

"A very long time. Some times are bound to really suck." His word reminded her of their previous conversation.

"Only, you can't back out, no matter how sucky things get."

He placed his lips on hers, tender, caring. "Say yes."

"I thought I already did."

Blake caught her in his arms and deepened their promising kiss. The headache and heartache of the last several days started to fade, and a flutter swelled deep inside her stomach.

Samantha gasped and pulled away from Blake's kiss.

"What is it?" he asked, alarmed.

"The baby. I felt the baby." She waited, placed a hand over her stomach, and felt the fluttering sensation again. She grasped Blake's hand, but knew the movement was too tiny for him to feel.

"I think it's her way of saying she approves," Blake said against Sam's ear.

"Her? You think it's a girl?"

"Women are emotional creatures. Taking this time to show herself is her way of telling us to stay together."

Sam laughed. "You think so?"

"Maybe, or it's a boy and he's trying to kick some sense into both of us."

"Boy or girl, with us as parents, this child is bound to be pushy to have its needs met."

"I love you, Samantha."

As Blake lowered his lips to hers again, Samantha's only thought was of her love for her not-so-temporary husband.

Epilogue

They named their son Samuel Edmund Harrison. Samuel after Samantha, because Blake couldn't keep it in his pants and naming his child after Sam was something he was hell-bent on doing. And second, after his father, whom Blake just couldn't hate any longer since Edmund was the reason the two of them had met in the first place.

"You're such a greedy little earl, aren't you?" Samantha watched Eddie as he finished his afternoon meal. The doctor wasn't kidding when he said breast-fed infants ate every two hours. She didn't care. OK, if she were truthful, the middle-of-the-night feeding was weighing on her, but she still woke up every night and happily fed her son. Blake did his part by being on diaper duty and helping where he could. He tried staying awake in the beginning, but most nights fell asleep at her side as she met Eddie's needs.

Footsteps sounded in the master bedroom and carried closer to the nursery.

Blake stood in the doorway with a silly smile on his face. "I thought I'd find the two of you in here."

Eddie heard his father's voice and smiled around Sam's nipple. "Do you hear your daddy?"

Blake stepped into the room and knelt down beside the rocker. Eddie blinked his precious blue eyes and stopped sucking. "Perfect timing," Blake said as he reached for the burp cloth on Sam's shoulder and lifted their son into his arms.

She adjusted her clothing and noticed that Blake had changed from casual Saturday clothes to a suit and tie. "Do you have to go to the office?" It was their anniversary, and their intention was to stay home for a quiet dinner.

"What husband would go to work on his first wedding anniversary?"

Eddie let out a good burp.

"Exactly," Blake said.

"Then why the change?"

"I have a surprise."

Sam stood and narrowed her eyes. "What kind of surprise?"

"You'll see."

He took her hand and led her down the stairs and into the formal living room.

The smell of flowers arrested her nose before she walked in. Then she saw them. Blake's mother and Gwen, Jordan and the personal nurse they'd hired to care for her in their home, Carter, Eliza, and all of their house staff. "What's going on?"

"Surprise!" Jordan waved from her wheelchair.

"I thought surprise parties were only for birthdays, not anniversaries."

Linda moved to Blake's side. "Where is my

beautiful grandson?" She took Eddie from Blake's arms, leaned over, and kissed both Samantha's cheeks in greeting.

Blake tucked Samantha into his arm. "They are all here for more than just an anniversary party."

"They are?"

"Yep. They're here for a wedding."

Now she was confused.

Sam looked around the room and didn't see anyone paired up. Carter, Gwen, and Eliza were the only young eligibles in the room, and they were positioned far apart from one another.

"Who?"

"Us."

"OK, I know pregnancy fried a few of my brain cells, but last I checked, we're already married."

Blake leaned forward and kissed the confusion away. When he lifted his lips from hers, he explained. "Last year we deprived all of our friends and family of witnessing our elopement. We both know the reason as to why . . . But I don't want anyone to question my love for you ever again. From this anniversary forward, we are going to renew our vows in a different state each year."

Sam displayed her guppy mouth. "Every year?"

"Isn't that romantic?" Gwen asked at her side.

"And when we run out of states, we'll move on to Europe."

A crazy rush of tears gathered behind Sam's eyes

as she stared at her incredible, loving husband. "You're nuts. You know that, right?"

"I used more choice words than that," Carter said.

"Don't use them now. There's a baby in the room." Eliza waved a finger in Carter's direction and was met with a wink.

"A wedding on each anniversary?"

Blake nodded once. "As simple or elaborate as you wish. Every other year, one of us plans it, or maybe we'll give the job to someone else to figure out."

Gwen clapped her hands. "Oh, I want next year. I have the perfect theme for a Texas wedding."

"Themes?"

"I'll take Hawaii on your fifth," Eliza chimed in.

Oh Lord, this crackpot group was jumping in feetfirst. Much like she did when she'd said *I do* to Blake the first time.

"What the heck. I'm in."

"That's my girl." Blake pulled her closer, the heat and comfort of his arms wound around her like a blanket.

"I'll tell the minister we're almost ready," Eliza said as she walked away.

"I'll check on the caterer." Mary started toward the kitchen.

"When did you plan all of this?" Sam asked as their family and friends filed out of the room.

"You and Eddie nap a lot."

Sam laughed and, shortly after, tried hiding a yawn behind her hand. "The doctor said Eddie should be sleeping through the night by the third month."

Blake kissed her forehead. "Just don't fall asleep before you say 'I do.'"

Samantha placed her palm on the side of Blake's face and lifted up on her tiptoes. "Oh, I do! A thousand times over, I do!" Then she sealed her vow with a butterfly-inducing kiss.

Acknowledgments

I have to take a moment and send a big publishing hug to Crystal Posey—aka the goddess of all things website and book covers. I know you were apprehensive about the whole book cover gig, but man, did you come through with this one. *Thank you* is such a paltry phrase for my appreciation of all you do.

As always, a big thanks to my critique partner Sandra Stixrude—aka Angel Martinez. Without your editorial eye, publishing this book wouldn't have been possible.

One more shout-out to my Facebook friends and fans who helped me come up with the title for this book. God, I love social media.

About the Author

New York Times bestselling author Catherine Bybee was raised in Washington State, but after graduating high school, she moved to Southern California in hopes of becoming a movie star. After growing bored with waiting tables, she returned to school and became a registered nurse, spending most of her career in urban emergency rooms. She now writes full-time and has penned the novels *Married by Monday* and *Not Quite Dating*. Bybee lives with her husband and two teenage sons in Southern California.

Center Point Large Print
600 Brooks Road / PO Box 1
Thorndike, ME 04986-0001 USA

(207) 568-3717

US & Canada:
1 800 929-9108
www.centerpointlargeprint.com